FINAL STRIKE

THE JUSTICE TRILOGY BOOK THREE

STEPHEN MERTZ

ROUGH
EDGES
PRESS

PRAISE FOR STEPHEN MERTZ

"A Grandmaster of action/adventure novels!
—MensAdventureMagazines&Books.com

"One of the best adventure writers of our time!"
—James M. Reasoner

"Stephen Mertz writes a hard-edged, fast-paced thriller for those who like their tales straight and sharp!"
—Joe R. Lansdale

"The cleanest, strongest prose in the business!"
—Gravetapping.com

"The Mertz Formula: rousing action and an exciting plot!"
—Prof. Wm. H. Young, A Study of Adventure Fiction

"One of the best writers in the genre!"
—Max Allan Collins

Final Strike
Paperback Edition
© Copyright 2022 Stephen Mertz

Rough Edges Press
An Imprint of Wolfpack Publishing
5130 S. Fort Apache Rd. 215-380
Las Vegas, NV 89148

roughedgespress.com

Paperback ISBN 978-1-68549-074-4
LCCN 2022935615

FINAL STRIKE

CHAPTER ONE

CODY LEANED out the passenger window of the speeding taxicab and triggered off three rounds from the Beretta.

The slugs pierced the windshield of the first pursuit vehicle, a rust-mottled pickup truck, and the head of its driver. The vehicle, sprouting a crew of wildly-firing gunmen, went into a crazy skid before crashing into a concrete highway divider, erupting in a ball of fire. There were three other trucks behind it, each one filled with gunmen intent on taking down Cody and the cab – preferably both. He had been in Syria exactly fifteen minutes and already the mission had turned bad.

He gripped the rear of the front seat and leaned toward the driver. "We need to get off the highway!"

"Turn off just ahead!" the driver, Hamid Hassan, replied without turning, his bald, tanned head nodding. "Another minute or less!"

Bullets drummed the roof like steel rain. "How much farther?"

"Quarter mile!"

Outside, the brown and mottled cityscape of Damascus flashed by. The country was hardly a garden spot but his hunt for Thelma Justice and Greb Vetrov had brought him here. His intel had confirmed that Vetrov, a former Russian general, was trafficking stolen nuclear weapons and Thelma Justice was his best customer. The international media darling – author, self-help guru and women's rights advocate – had recently taken a leap from the top of the Nielsen ratings to the top of Homeland Security's terror watch list. Cody had come to remove her from the list. His CIA partner Sara Durell, meanwhile, was working in parallel in France. Cody intended to deliver on his piece of the mission.

Provided he lived.

He shot a look back over his shoulder. The three remaining trucks were bobbing and weaving in and out of traffic behind them, the men standing in their beds blasting AK fire indiscriminately in his direction, oblivious to traffic. Strangely, the local drivers didn't seem much perturbed by the bullets. Cody wondered if they were just another inconvenience of the morning commute in Damascus. Given the dictatorial regime, the recent Russian occupation and the various jihadi nut-jobs populating the region, that made sense.

He switched sides, leaned out the window and blasted off three more shots.

He had arrived incognito aboard an Air France flight, using a false passport identifying him as a French civil engineer linked to an NGO in the region. There were plenty of NGOs in the Middle East – a few of them even legitimate. It should have been a relatively straightforward insertion: false papers, believable cover, civilian flight, friendly contact waiting at the airport. But very little had been straightforward for

Cody since getting entangled in a web of stolen nuclear weapons and international terrorism. Upon his arrival, operatives of Crimson Jihad, the group rumored to be prepping a stunt involving WMDs, had been lying in wait.

The Beretta clicked. Cody's high rate of fire had caused a jam. He turned to the driver.

"I need a gun!" he snapped.

Hamid reached down into the passenger leg well and dragged up a battered and dusty carpetbag by the handles that he pushed over the seat to Cody. Swerving to avoid a clutch of pedestrians who scattered in shrieks, he said: "Look inside!"

Hamid Hassan was the latest in a series of contacts he and his partner Sara Durell had used in their pursuit of Justice and Vetrov. As far as CIA was concerned, Cody and Sara were off the reservation – rogue operatives acting without official sanction. This lack of support was offset by an informal network of retired agents called Backchannel who were known to provide assistance to agents in the field. Parsons, their leader, was a Brit living in Moscow. Jacquard, their French contact, had been killed, but not before handing off Cody to Hamid Hassan.

He parted the carpetbag's clasp and peered down into a disorderly jumble of munitions and small arms: revolvers, automatics, hand grenades and two partially disassembled, old-timey Thompson machine-guns with drum barrels. The bag looked like it had been stolen from the back of Al Capone's closet.

"Here! We get off highway!" Hamid pumped the brakes, jerked the wheel and sent them hurtling down an off-ramp toward a crowded parking lot. Cody caught sight of a billboard depicting a roller coaster and a clown.

The red Arabic script presumably said something about an amusement park.

"What the hell are you doing?" Cody pawed through the bag for a weapon. Behind them, the pickups were taking the off-ramp and pursuing them, coming in hot.

"Biggest amusement park in Syria!" Hamid spoke calmly despite the challenge of navigating a cab at terminal velocity. "Should be full this morning! Is national holiday!"

Cody studied the road ahead. "You're boxing us in! This road dead-ends into a parking lot!"

"I know, friend Cody! Is chance to lose these assholes!" Despite the desperate situation, the seventy-something Palestinian driver cackled at Cody in the rear-view mirror. "You watch! I used to drive for Mossad! The lot is like Tel Aviv during rush hour!"

With a massive thrust of his shoulders, he wrenched the wheel and the cab – an old Ford sedan – spun at a ninety-degree angle before plunging between the gate posts and down a row of parked vehicles.

Cody steadied himself by grabbing the chicken bar. "You're planning to lose them?"

"No!" Hamid slowed slightly, jabbing the brakes. "I set them up! You eliminate them!"

"Okay! Just…watch out for civilians!"

"*Inshallah!* Allah is compassionate and merciful! He is on our side!"

The guys chasing us believe the same thing, Cody thought, rooting through the bag.

The pickup trucks meanwhile had swerved through the gate and into the lot behind them. Cody heard the rattle of AK fire. Pedestrians hit the deck. That's when he perceived the method behind Hassan's madness.

Most of these cars are empty and any civilians caught in

the open can shelter behind them, he thought. Crouching behind two layers of steel and an engine block made them safer than the drivers through whom they'd just been chased on the highway.

Hassan swung the wheel. They skidded around the end of one row of cars before plunging down another. One of the pickups switched direction to intercept them.

"Company's coming!" cried Cody. He grabbed up a Thompson, secured the breech and jammed a drum into the feeder. The bolt moved smoothly enough for an antique weapon. He prayed the thing still worked.

The pickup truck had appeared at the end of the row and set a course to intercept. Cody rolled down the window. "Covering fire in ten seconds!" he warned.

"Truck coming! Head on at full speed! Let's see who is bigger chicken, eh?"

"Good plan!" said Cody, although he wasn't exactly sold on the idea.

AK fire blazed from the oncoming truck. Hassan, all confidence and kamikaze spirit, stepped on the gas, aiming dead center for the onrushing vehicle's engine block. Cody grasped the Thompson and leaned out the window, sighting on the approaching driver.

He squeezed the trigger and the old weapon snarled to life in his hands like a pneumatic rattlesnake. Hot lead streamed from the pug-snout barrel and blasted out part of the grill and the left-front headlight. The AK rifleman behind the driver ducked. The one behind the passenger seat didn't and switched his aim to Cody. A second later, he came on with his next burst.

The bullets bounced off the hood. Cody regripped the stock of the Thompson. The two vehicles were one hundred yards apart and closing. He gritted his teeth and returned fire. That burst cut the driver in half.

The truck's windshield imploded, collapsing under the salvo. The nose swerved left, right and left again. The rifleman behind the driver was pitched out. And the guy on the left dropped his gun to grip the cab roof. The thing finally ended up ploughing straight into a concrete barrier and bursting into flames. Hamid crowed with laughter as they sped past.

"Nice shooting, man!"

"The other truck! It's circling around!"

"I see! I see!"

The next truck had swerved into the row beside theirs, one car length away but coming up alongside at a brisk clip. They would draw level with the taxi in a matter of seconds.

Cody reached into the bag and grasped one of the grenades. It was an antique – an old-style pineapple grenade from World War II, complete with a spoon handle and cotter pin. Cody yanked the pin, prayed it still worked, leaned out the window and hurled the grenade like he was flinging a pigskin to a wide receiver in a crucial play in the last quarter of a championship game, one where everything depended on it landing right.

And it did.

Arcing over the cars between them to land in the truck bed, the grenade mushroomed in a geyser of cordite and flame, a ballooning envelope of fire that reduced everything within it to shreds.

"Good arm!" Hamid grinned fiercely. "You play baseball?"

"Football!"

"We got one more truck!"

Cody scanned. "Where?"

"Coming up behind!"

Cody hit the seat a moment before the rear window collapsed under a hail of AK fire. He jammed a fresh drum magazine into the Thompson, sat up and fired a volley through the shattered mouth of the rear window. Bullets punched into the hood of the truck behind. He saw oil gust up through one hole and the engine buck. The truck stalled and fell back, its engine suddenly seizing.

"*Allahua-ackbar!*" Hamid's delight was palpable. He shifted gears and stepped on the accelerator.

"We should regroup and debrief," said Cody. "You got a safehouse?"

"I have my house! Is low profile, very safe!" Hamid steered back toward the highway. "You be my guest!"

"I'd be honored." Cody gave a weary smile. Hamid was alright.

CHAPTER TWO

WITH A HEART-STOPPING SQUEAL OF BRAKES, Hamid
Hassan jerked to a halt by a wooden fence in a back alley
of Damascus. Cody found himself releasing breath he
hadn't known he was holding. He realized he would be
more comfortable HALO jumping from a C-130 in the
middle of a thunderstorm than he would ever riding in
this man's cab again. When it came to driving, Hamid
Hassan was an absolute terror.

The world beyond the wooden fence was even more
unusual.

One moment, Cody was in a Damascus street, facing
something very like a construction fence. The next he
was passing through a veil of palm fronds and bamboo
shoots into a junkyard that was a sculpture garden of the
past thirty years of global conflict. Cody had heard of
"junk" artists before, men who transformed the twisted
metal of automobile wrecks or abandoned construction
projects into modern works of art. But what Hamid
Hassan kept in his back yard took the state of the art to a
whole new level.

Here was a free-standing impression of an elephant with its truck extended. Except its trunk was the discarded canon of a T-72 tank such as many a Russian left behind in Afghanistan. Over there was a surreal representation of a stork and her children fashioned from a Chinese rocket launcher. A rack of rifles had been refashioned into a giant rack of ribs that looked like something Fred Flintstone might eat. It turned out Hamid was something of an artist of war.

The Palestinian led Cody through the steel jungle to a shack at its center. He guessed this must be Hamid's workshop. A series of clamps lined a workbench. A welder's portable blowtorch sat in a rack at one end. And a clutch of unfinished art projects crowded the space like wallflowers cluttering up a church dance floor. No sooner did he arrive than Hamid seized up something resembling a steel butterfly and began fiddling with it.

"Thanks for the lift from the airport."

"Sure! Sure thing!"

"How much did Jacquard tell you?"

"Jacquard?"

Cody swallowed a knot of frustration. "Jacquard. The Backchannel agent who put me onto you."

"Backchannel? Sure, sure." With a crash, Hamid let what it was he was holding drop to the workbench. "Frenchman say you coming. That is all."

"That's it?"

"He send initial briefing by e-mail." Hamid shrugged. "Promised to follow up but he was killed."

"Yes. I was there." Cody fought down a cold dagger of anger at the men responsible. "I'm here looking for someone—"

"At your service!" Hamid cried, pulling on a set of

welding goggles. "If he is in Damascus, Hamid will help you find him. Who is?"

"The man I'm looking for is the leader of a terrorist movement called Crimson Jihad. He's involved in dealings with a man named Vetrov, a Russian officer who sells stolen nukes."

At this, Hamid abruptly stopped and turned, dark visors swallowing his eyes, an unlit welding gun in his fist. "You mean the White Wolf? You looking for him?"

"That's right. The one they sometimes call 'the Imam'. You know him?"

Hamid Hassan began to swear, a rich line of curse words that rattled with menace. Even though he didn't understand every word, the meaning was clear. Cody doubted he had heard cursing that bad since boot camp. "White Wolf is completely insane, man. He imagine he be like ancient folk hero from Crusades. He behave like Medieval warlord. Behead people and like that. Hamid want nothing to do with him."

"Well, of course not. You just have to tell me how to find him."

"I don't know. That…is a lot to ask, friend Cody." Hamid's mouth flattened into a hard line. "You will need to enter the desert. Is very dangerous."

"I need to find him, Hamid. Can you help me?"

"Can Hamid help you find your own death? Sure." He flicked a thumb back over his shoulder. "Go back to airport. The White Wolf found you there. You return, he will find you again. Must have known you were coming. Why you want to find the White Wolf?"

"My concern is his connection to Greb Vetrov. Did Jacquard brief you on him?"

"No." Hamid began sorting through a box of tools. "He tell me only that American agents coming and ask me to help. So you come but you only one agent. And he say nothing about suicide project."

"Suicide didn't seem to bother you back there in the parking lot," Cody pointed out.

"Hamid did not know those were Crimson Jihad." He shrugged.

"Would that have made a difference?"

"No." He paused and removed his welder's goggles. "Jacquard was my friend. One time in Baghdad, he save my life. We make deal to help each other. He send you. You want help? Okay. But Crimson Jihad...those boys are crazy."

Cody smiled. "My thoughts, exactly."

At least they agreed on that.

———

Syria, Hamid explained, had been on its way to healing until the White Wolf appeared.

It had never been a happy place. A dictator dad had been succeeded by his dictator son and more of the same ensued. Syria was a moderately Muslim country, with the same sort of modern infrastructure as Saudi Arabia or Jordan. But a repressive police state, shiftless malcontents, a rebel movement and diplomatic chaos combined to create the perfect storm. First the Americans, then the Russians and then finally ISIS. One after another, they paraded across Syria's stage, wreaking havoc in their wake. Even the normally gullible tribesmen were wary of anyone selling salvation.

The Imam had arrived as part of that storm. There are certain men, Hamid claimed, who profited from chaos, men that were able somehow to master the currents and ride the waves of insanity to power. Hitler was one. The White Wolf, who took the name 'Imam', was another.

"They say he study theology." Hamid rummaged on his work bench until he found a silver tea kettle, which he filled from a tap and placed on the heat ring of a propane stove. "Was preparing to be religious leader until he discover he have other talents. Put down his Q'uran for an AK-47."

His movement gained traction quickly among the illiterate tribesmen of the northeast, groups accustomed to being pushed around by the Syrians on one side, the Kurds on the other and whichever military contractor happened to be stomping around at any given time. The White Wolf had discovered and stoked their discontent. Beneath his skilled ministrations, that anger blossomed into a movement.

"You know who White Wolf really admire?" Hamid was rummaging in a drawer now for tea.

"Osama bin-Laden?"

"Bill Gates." Hamid adjusted the flame on the heat ring. "He speak of global initiatives, of solving big problems. Bill Gates do it with vaccines and computers. The White Wolf do it with Islam."

"So his focus is global?"

"He has plan, yes." Hamid spread his arms. "Big plans! White Wolf believe time has come for worldwide caliphate. He say *sharia* will solve all the problems of inequality, racism, poverty, et cetera, et cetera."

"Well, he's ambitious. I'll give him that." Cody reached into a pocket of his utility jacket and drew out a map. "This part of the country here is supposed to be his area of operations. Do you have any idea where his base might be located?"

Hamid squinted at the page. "Yes, that is his ballpark. His base probably somewhere … here." He jabbed with a stubby finger. "These villages in the highlands. He favors those tribes. They are important recruiting grounds for his soldiers."

"His ideology catches on with the locals, does it?"

"Sure." Hamid shrugged. "He is very charismatic. In his vision of the world, the poor will be rich, and the rich will be brought low. Justice of Allah will prevail, and all will be perfect and fair."

"Sounds appealing."

"All that is required is two things: destruction of Christianity and destruction of capitalism." Hamid spotted steam rising from the kettle and fetched cups. "Once that happen, the White Wolf say everything be wonderful."

CHAPTER THREE

2500 MILES from Cody's position, on a highway heading north through rural France, Sara Durell heard the chirp of her encrypted phone receiving a text and pulled over into a lay-by. She had been expecting word from Cody in Syria and was pleased to see the message was from him. She gave the pull-out and washrooms a careful visual scan, ensuring she was completely alone before opening her text messages.

Arrived, Syria. In contact with Backchannel. Good background on target, working to locate. Anticipating rendezvous with V soon.

Sara texted back:

Still tracking our missing cub. Trail leads to Paris. Heading there now.

She pressed SEND, stowed her phone back in her

pocket and pulled back onto the highway, heading north.

A seasoned veteran of CIA, Sara Durell was accustomed to throwing herself in harm's way for the good of her country. But she ordinarily did this with the full assistance of the Agency and its global web of contacts and material support behind her. But for now, she and Cody were on their own.

What had begun as mere curiosity on Sara's part had landed her in the middle of a complex web of nuclear terrorism and religious extremism. Everything had started with a young woman – an Emirati princess named Aisha bint al-Ahmad. Her sudden appearance in the United States, alone and without any sort of official escort, had come to Sara's attention and piqued her curiosity. The young noblewoman had come to Washington DC to attend a rally by female empowerment guru Thelma Justice. Sara had stepped off the Agency reservation by going to shadow the princess on her own, without alerting her superiors. The results had been disastrous.

After being injured during a violent confrontation at the rally between Thelma Justice's security force and a group led by the princess' brother, Sara had begun to perceive the outlines of a partnership that suggested a massive criminal conspiracy. Princess Aisha had wandered into an arrangement between Thelma Justice and a man named Greb Vetrov, a former Russian general who had decided to go into business for himself selling off bits of Russia's old nuclear deterrent. Jack Cody had intercepted one such shipment on its way to North Korea. Another was now on its way to Syria.

After another try by the princess' brother to bring her home against her will, Cody had rescued Aisha and, along with Sara, the three of them had cooperated to frustrate the alliance between Thelma Justice and Greb Vetrov. But then Aisha had done the same thing to Cody and Sara that she'd done to her family – abandoned them to seek answers on her own.

What had drawn Aisha to Thelma Justice was a combination of two factors. The first was Thelma's role as an advocate for gender equality and global justice. The second was the fragment Aisha had in her possession.

That damn fragment...

Sara blinked, her vision blurring with fatigue and road hypnosis. She needed to pause and refuel, rest up before pushing the rest of the way to Paris. Seeing a roadside diner ahead, she pulled into the lot, cut the engine of the rental car and took a table inside near the back. She ordered coffee and a breakfast platter. When the java arrived, she drew out her cellphone and scrolled to her photo gallery. There she found a snapshot of the antique relic at the heart of this mess.

It was a simple clay tablet, nothing more. And yet the number of deaths the relic had occasioned – the number of times it had been discovered, stolen, rediscovered, killed for, fought over, lost and found again – were legion. Sara knew the contents of the tablet, was aware of its controversial message and understood Princess Aisha's ambivalence about keeping the thing to herself versus giving it to someone like Thelma Justice.

Poor girl grew up in a man's world. A... 'patriarchal' world. She grimaced, thinking of the word as she sipped her java. Feminism had ceased to interest her as anything more than an academic exercise. *Muslim scholars have their view of the tablet. The Catholic Church has its view. The one perspective we never hear from is...*

Her meal came. She closed the photo, thanked the

waitress and stuffed a Bluetooth earphone into place. She toggled her cellphone to the audiobooks portal she had accessed as part of her background research on the relic. With a click of her thumb, she resumed listening to *Massacre at the Samarian Hills: A Mystery of the Second Crusade* by E.A. Peart, PhD. The narrator's voice drifted up and interposed itself between Sara and the background noise of the diner and the highway traffic outside.

> … *observing, for the most part, the knightly virtues generally recognized by both the Christian and Muslim soldiers of the period. Departures from chivalric norms became rarer as both sides refined the expectations for training and comportment of their troops. The event in the Samarian Hills proved to be a notable enough departure to occasion objection from leadership on both sides (both sides as the side responsible for the action remained in question).*
>
> *What is not in question is that on or around the morning of 2 December 1149, a column of troops approached a Samaritan village. Preparations had been underway for a wedding in the village. The suddenness and savagery with which the village was attacked and the resulting slaughter were unprecedented, even under the brutal terms of Crusader warfare …*

Sara finished her eggs and toast, washing them down with a mouthful of coffee. She was soon glad she had eaten first before reading this next bit.

> *The absolute brutality of the attack and the punishments inflicted upon the civilian population were barbaric, even by the standards of the time. Entire families were*

butchered and dumped in the culverts. Men in particular were singled out, with portions of their anatomy removed and hung from gates and rooftops. Women were cut open and their innards removed. Children and babies were massacred in the cradle. Gruesome images were painted on the walls of houses by the attackers – strange symbols that priests of the time deemed Satanic. And is it any wonder, given the brutal and horrific nature of the attack?

Somehow the clay tablet, the relic Aisha had found, had figured prominently in the massacre. The tablet itself was carried for a time in a messenger bag Aisha kept slung over one shoulder – a bag into which was sewn the tracking device Sara now followed. The tablet had been secreted someplace safe. The messenger bag remained. So it was only a matter of time before she caught up with the princess…

But the mental images of the massacre would not leave her. Although more rest would have been nice, before she knew it, Sara was rising and paying her bill, anxious to get back on the road.

Pulling onto the highway, she wondered what it was about religious extremism that prompted such insanity. She had been raised to be a good Episcopalian, attending the same sort of church patronized by most of the white power elites in Washington. Was it poverty and privation that prompted the hellish violence? It occurred to her that you were more likely to find high church types at fundraisers or on the golf-course than in the front lines of a holy war.

When people are desperate, she thought, *they cling to God. And the more desperate they are, the tighter they cling.*

She produced the pager-sized tracker that was homed

in on the tracking device sewn into the lining of Aisha's messenger bag. A similar desperation had prompted the girl's flight into the arms of Thelma Justice and the Order of World Harmony, and a similar insanity infused that organization. Sara hoped she wasn't too late.

CHAPTER FOUR

AT THAT VERY MOMENT, Thelma Justice stood in her office in the Paris headquarters of the Order of World Harmony. Before her, perched in an adjustable cradle, was a marvellously-wrought globe of the Earth. A wonder of the cartographer's art, her globe could be swiveled to any preferred vantage with the toggle of a joystick and any one of the nations and its major cities lit up at the press of a button on the control console. In the early evening light, with the offices and corridors of her organization now quiet, she was free to examine this expensive model and finally make use of it for the next phase of her and Greb Vetrov's plan.

A light tapping sounded on the partially opened door behind her. Windy Duke, her personal assistant, took a hesitant step into the room and spoke.

"Ms. Justice, you asked to see us?"

"Windy, yes." Thelma Justice looked up with a pleasant smile. "I hope you brought some help."

"I did." Windy Duke turned and motioned for the woman in the hallway to join her. Thelma Justice recognized her as one of the new interns. "Ms. Justice, this is Lenore. She just joined the organization."

"Hello, Lenore. The both of you please come in. And close the door behind you, would you please? Thanks."

Windy Duke, accompanied by Lenore, a smooth-skinned young Senegalese woman in her twenties, entered the office. After closing the door, Windy switched on a white noise baffle Thelma Justice had ordered installed to prevent people from listening in from the outside.Her boss has indicated that this evening's meeting was to address projects of a highly proprietary and confidential nature. Once she saw that both women were settled and had their notepads at the ready, Thelma Justice began.

"I'm initiating a series of projects on a global scale," she said. "This will involve coordination of numerous initiatives, all of which will be coordinated through our office in Damascus. All of this has to dovetail precisely within the next few days. I am hoping I can count on you to arrange it."

"Yes, Ms. Justice," said Windy Duke, her head down at her notepad.

"Excellent." Thelma Justice touched a button on the globe's control panel and the sphere rotated to expose the Middle East, with Syria outlined in red and its capital identified by a winking white light. "Damascus will serve as the preliminary hub, but the span of the final project will be global. We'll need to coordinate numerous factors.

"First, I'm going to need you to set up a front company, Windy. An international courier service. Nothing too in-depth – a website, a logo, a bank account. None of it traceable to us, of course. But you'll need a name and the ability to lease commercial carrier jets. We'll probably need about eight or ten. The jets and pilots will be leased for a period of two weeks to ferry materials and personnel out of Syria. Our start date is next Wednesday."

She glanced over at the two women, both busily scribbling on their notepads.

"These flights will be going to the capitals of the following nations." She touched another button and a series of countries shimmered into visibility. "Greece. Italy. Germany. France, of course. Czechoslovakia. Poland. England..."

Windy Duke scribbled furiously, checking to ensure Lenore was keeping up. Between the two of them, they would get the entire list and double-check it.

"I will need you to book hotel rooms in each destination. Make them nice, large chain hotels. Anonymous. Book each room for two weeks. Arrange with the hotel staff to provide room service meals twice daily for two weeks to each room. Get the keys in advance. Arrange to have the keys, an envelope of local currency in the equivalent of $100 US and a few changes of men's clothing placed in a suitcase and the suitcase itself secured within a storage locker in the airport of the given capital. Once the suitcases and their contents are secured within each storage locker, have the keys collected and forwarded to our people in Damascus. You with me so far?"

"Yes, ma'am," said Windy Duke. "Airport storage lockers. Suitcases inside containing hotel room keys, cash, change of clothing. In those cities."

Thelma Justice thought for a moment. "Make sure the hotels are identified. Say, a note taped to each key. Have the name and number of the reserved room written on each in Arabic."

"Will do, ma'am."

"I'll need the following items delivered to our headquarters in Syria in addition to the locker keys. Fifty identical black lunchboxes, the kind you see construction workers use. I'll also need fifty burner cellphones. They won't need any call plan or special features. Just the ability to take incoming calls. These phones will be used exactly once, then discarded. So nothing expensive. Register the phones with the local area code of each of the national capitals I've identified."

Lenore and Windy noted this down.

"And fifty orange jumpsuits. Have each patched with the logo of the fake courier service. Size medium. Send these to Damascus as well."

"Will do."

Thelma Justice smiled. "Any questions, ladies?"

Windy and Lenore shared a look. Neither had any questions. Both shook their heads.

"This needs to be done quickly and quietly." Thelma Justice emphasized this by rapping twice on the globe's console. "Nobody else involved but you two. Set yourselves up in Catherine's old office. Get a locking file cabinet and store your notebooks, files and any paperwork related to the project inside. Arrange a Fury to stand guard outside the room twenty-four seven. Nobody gets in but you. I want you to get started immediately and report to me the moment you're done."

As one, the two assistants rose and made for the hall, closing the door behind them.

Thelma Justice turned back to the globe.

Hers was a women's organization. What had begun as a female empowerment initiative had grown over time to become a multinational corporation. That success was a testament to the power of women, to the inevitability of their eventual triumph. Women were, plainly and simply, *superior* to men. It was time for them to move to the forefront and assert their natural leadership over the world and its affairs.

Hers was a women's organizations. Soon, it would be a women's world.

CHAPTER FIVE

HEAD DOWN, shoulders hunched, arms clutching her messenger bag to her side, Princess Aisha bint al-Ahmad hurried through the narrow streets of Montmartre, trying hard not to look over her shoulder.

She had experienced genuine relief upon arrival in Paris. Before that, she, Cody and Sara had been in Monte Carlo – a target for trouble from Greb Vetrov, Thelma Justice and representatives of the Vatican. All had been interested in the clay tablet Aisha carried – a First-Century document of geopolitical significance. Somehow, that tablet was central to an unfolding plot involving stolen nuclear weapons and the Order of World Harmony. That people had been willing to kill for the tablet made Aisha's decision to abandon Cody and Sara all the more attractive.

They're safer without me, she'd told herself.

The tablet she had tucked away someplace safe – the private safety deposit box she kept at her bank in Zurich. In the meantime, she needed some guidance on what to do with the relic. Cody's and Sara's advice would be politically motivated. Her family's advice would be religiously motivated. Neither, she thought, would place the general welfare of the world above the self-interest of competing power cohorts. And so she had come to Paris, where the Order of World Harmony had its European headquarters.

She needed to talk to Thelma Justice.

But first she had to get rid of the man that was following her.

He had struck up a conversation with Aisha upon her arrival at le Gare de Nord. There on the platform he had seemed harmless enough, just an elderly Parisian man – a little sad and overweight. In his cloth cap and windbreaker, he looked like a dozen other retirees common to urban areas. She had been polite to the man, chatted for a minute then made her excuses and departed. As she had walked away, he said something she hadn't been ale to make out. She just kept walking, pretending not to hear …

That's when his voice came again, raised this time in anger. He started following her, repeating his question. Now, half-an-hour later, he was still following and gave no sign of stopping. If anything, he seemed more determined.

"*Madamoiselle!*" he cried. "*Attendez-vous, s'il vous plait!*"

Miss, please wait for me. *Why?* Aisha turned a corner onto a deserted street of closed shops. It was almost six PM, and the sun was setting on a city shutting down at the end of the business day. There was nowhere to seek refuge in amongst the locked buildings and empty cafes. That's when her eyes seized on the public toilets.

The *pissoirs* of old Paris were gradually being removed or refurbished into co-ed public washrooms. The one she saw was about the size of a garden shed, with separate entrances for men and women. Breathing a prayer of thanks, she ducked into the latter, found a stall and closed the door. A minute later, she heard the man's angry footsteps click past. *"Ou etes vous?"* he demanded to know, wondering where she had gone. She sat holding her breath until the footsteps vanished into the distance.

Safe. For now.

Aisha sighed and unlocked the stall. She was trembling. Unsteadily, she went to the one sink in the washroom and turned on the faucet. Moiling her hands in the greasy soap from the public dispenser, she washed up and used the blow dryer to finish. The machine had just clicked off when her ears twitched...

The angry footsteps were back, heading in this direction!

She dashed back to the stall, closed and locked the door and drew her feet up from the floor so it looked unoccupied. Her hand closed around the knife in her coat pocket.

"Aaaa – llo? Allo? Mon petite? Vous etes la?"

Hello, hello, my little one. Are you there? Aisha composed herself with some deep breathing, drew the knife and waited.

Now the footsteps had entered the women's washroom. He was going down the stalls and pushing open the doors one by one, questioning in a sing-song voice if she was in...*this* one? No. Perhaps...*this* one? No...

He suspected she was here. And he was playing with her.

"Vous etes...la?"

The door to the stall next to hers crashed open. The man sighed. Stepped toward the closed door of Aisha's and pushed...

Click.

Locked.

The man started to laugh. He knew he had her now. Confident the quarry was near and vulnerable, he shifted his feet and started to kneel, lowering first one knee and then the other in the manner of stiff, older men. Then his hands came down. Next, his face would appear beneath the stall door, and she would be caught.

She never gave him the chance.

Lunging forward, she ripped open the stall door to confront the kneeling man. Startled, he looked up in time to see her knife descend. Aisha stabbed and withdrew, stabbed and withdraw until he stopped screaming. Then she was off and running, out through the washroom door and back into the night.

CHAPTER SIX

In the mountains of northeast Syria, Selim Farah Mohammed, the man known as the White Wolf, stood brooding at the edge of a forbidding mountain pass, troubled by apocalyptic visions.

The visions had tormented him since boyhood – visions of fire and carnage, of wrecked cities and piled bodies. If the White Wolf closed his eyes, he could see great mountains of skeletons rising to the heavens, packing the world with a stench to make the senses rebel and the heart run cold with horrors. It wasn't until he left his home village for university, not until he was an ambitious young student in Damascus that the answer came. Late one night, alone in his room, tormented by these visions, he crashed to his knees in prayer, asking for relief. That's when he knew…

Allah had chosen him.

Out of the millions in his home country, out of the thousands of university students – many of whom were wealthier and more educated than the White Wolf himself – he alone had been selected to receive visions of the fiery end Allah had planned for the world. At the time, he had been tormented by this. Why had God chosen him? Now, many years later, he understood with a clarity that put everything in perspective. The world was unclean.

It needed to be renewed by fire.

He had withdrawn from university, disgusted by the selfish decadence of his fellow undergraduates. He had returned to his village and thrown himself into its work with a will. While his former fellows at the university spent Friday nights at movies and in night clubs, the White Wolf was to be found in the simple mosque of his village, leaning close to every word uttered by the *imam*. He had to understand how Allah wanted him to serve. Assisting in the daily work and extending that day by offering his back in service to the widows and orphans among his people was not enough. Selim Farah Mohammed wanted to step directly into the flames and carnage of those visions. Now, standing above this mountain pass, he was about to get his chance.

The world built by the infidels was collapsing. Political turmoil, economic instability, pandemics and civil unrest had done their work. The once-proud civilizations of the west were tottering, the very sands shifting beneath their foundations. Soon the time would come for the warriors of Allah to strike, as they had of old.

The White Wolf would lead them.

A shifting of rock on the path behind alerted him to the presence of Mustafa, his second-in-command. A Nigerian, Mustafa had earned his spurs with Boko Haram where he had developed a reputation for cruelty and ruthlessness. He particularly took delight in punishing little girls who transgressed the observances of the strictest forms of radical Islam, such as by learning to read. He had left the bodies of many behind him in his homeland.

"Imam," said Mustafa, "I come with a report, as you requested."

The White Wolf tilted his head in Mustafa's direction. "Continue, most trusted one."

Mustafa approached, halting diffidently two steps behind his commander and speaking in respectful tones. "The test has been administered to every brother. The fifty most loyal and ruthless have been identified. They have been told to depart camp this night, under cover of dark, taking only the clothes on their backs and a rifle. They will assemble at sundown tomorrow at the base of the peak known as the Caliph's Tower."

"It is good." The White Wolf nodded, agreeing with himself. In the silence after, he felt something shift in Mustafa's mood and chuckled. "You have questions, Mustafa. Ask."

The White Wolf's subaltern was taken aback. It was not his commander's way to invite questions from his subordinates. But Mustafa considered anything the White Wolf said to be an order so he complied, unburdening himself of the concerns troubling him.

"Great One. I do not understand. Two days ago, you assembled the brothers and told them our movement was about to make a great stride forward in bringing the battle to the infidels. You spoke of the arrival of allies who would bring a great weapon – one you called the Hammer of God. You said all of these things would happen tomorrow. And yet now you instruct our fiercest and most loyal soldiers to depart under cover of night."

"You disagree?"

"Great One, it is not my place to agree or to disagree. I merely…" He shrugged. "I merely do not understand."

The White Wolf smiled. Mustafa's answer was perfect in its candor and loyalty. The White Wolf's love was reserved exclusively for Allah. But the warmth he felt for his loyal Nigerian general glowed, burning brightly as he gave his answer.

"As usual, my dearest disciple, you see right into the heart of the matter. To ask those loyal and effective fighters to depart is as strange an order as a commander has ever given on the eve of battle. But your loyalty proves that you understand this: that a soldier need not understand the reason for an order. It is his part to obey or disobey, as he sees fit."

"Yes, Great One."

"And so for this question – for your loyalty and candor, and concern for our movement – I shall reward you with a gift."

Mustafa bowed his head in gratitude, awaiting the gift. When it came, it surprised him.

"Mustafa, this night, under cover of darkness, you too will depart camp, taking only your rifle and the clothes on your back. You will rendezvous with the others at the Caliph's Tower. I will come to you at sundown, and all will be made clear."

"I await my commander's pleasure," Mustafa said. Without another word, he departed.

The White Wolf returned his attention to the valley and his apocalyptic visions.

CHAPTER SEVEN

GENERAL GREB VETROV gazed out the window of the helicopter as it chased its own shadow, which rippled and undulated across the dunes of the desert below. It was uncomfortably warm in the cabin of the Mi-17, and sunlight pierced the windows in a fiery blast. Vetrov, unequipped with the glare reducing optics worn by the Russian army pilot piloting the craft, had to squint whenever he looked toward the cockpit. The expected flying time from the Russian base outside of Damascus to the RV point was one hour. By Vetrov's watch, they should be nearing their destination.

His appearance at the base, in uniform and driving an official car, had caught the base commander off guard. Eager to be of service, the colonel had asked no questions of the general, accepting Vetrov's claim to be negotiating with friendly locals for logistic support of Russia's mission in the troubled country. The helicopter had been placed at his disposal along with an escort of armed soldiers. Vetrov had accepted the helicopter but demurred on the troops. He reassured the colonel he faced no danger.

And in truth, he did not. For the man he was going to see was a true confederate – a comrade in the old sense of the word. One to whom Vetrov had entrusted details of his plans.

"The landing coordinates are up ahead, G eneral." The pilot's voice was crisp in his earphones. "We're beginning our descent."

"Thank you," said Vetrov.

Vetrov had once flown in helicopters like the Mi-17 almost daily. In his former life as a commander of Russian nuclear forces and endgame strategist, he had had such a craft on call for his personal use 24 hours per day to inspect the far-flung outposts of Russia's nuclear deterrent. While still nominally attached to the Russian general staff, Vetrov had recently left the country. This was of concern to the senior levels of Russian leadership but not yet sufficiently so to order an all-out alert for him. This would change soon. But until then, Vetrov could use his reputation and rank to gain access to military assets to further his own purposes, as he was now doing.

A rock-strewn valley appeared within the sea of dunes below. The Mi-17 banked and came in for a landing at its edge. Two figures stood waiting, dressed in the robes of desert dwellers.

Once the rotors stilled, Vetrov opened the hatch for himself and stepped down, the desert sand enveloping and warming his feet through his boots. The desert dwellers remained impassive during his approach, making not the slightest movement. They might just as well have been mirages. As Vetrov neared them, his ugly face beamed a wide smile.

"My friend, Selim!" He stopped before the taller of the two men and planted his hands on his hips. "It is good to see you again."

The White Wolf pushed aside the *keffiyeh* covering his lower face and spoke. *"Salaam aleikum,* Greb Vetrov. The enemy of my enemy is my friend."

They clasped forearms, desert fashion, and the White Wolf introduced his companion. "This is Mustafa, my second-in-command. Selim, this is General Greb Vetrov, our powerful ally from Russia."

"Salaam aleikum," said Mustafa.

"Mustafa goes now to gather with the fifty most loyal and dangerous of Crimson Jihad's followers." The White Wolf spoke next to Mustafa. "General Vetrov will help us lay a great blow to the enemies of the Prophet. Tell the men they are to consider him as equal to myself – worthy of respect and to be obeyed without question."

"I will, Great One." Mustafa bowed his head in obedience and then departed swiftly and silently across the sands to the valley below.

"Is everything planned for the morning?" The White Wolf's tone was its usual calm, controlled self. But Vetrov could read the worry in his eyes.

"It is, my friend. Do not fear." Vetrov laid a hand on the man's arm. "Everything has been arranged exactly as we discussed. All will go according to plan."

"And once the Cleansing is achieved?" The White Wolf glared down at Vetrov's hand until it was removed. "What then?"

"Then we move to the next phase of the operation. My operatives will move your men to cities across the west, both in Europe and the Americas. One man to each city. Each will be given a powerful sword to wield on our behalf. While they unleash chaos on the ground, the Hammer of God will descend from on high."

"Strong words," retorted the White Wolf. "I wonder if the actions will match their promise?"

"Absolutely." Vetrov, if he recognized the White Wolf's words as a jab, gave no sign. "We work or great purpose, you and I. Toward great ends. No details of the plan have been neglected. All will go as planned. You will see tomorrow."

"Tell me about the swords my men will be given." The White Wolf's attention piqued with the talk of weapons.

Smiling, Vetrov reached into a pocket and produced a sealed glass vial perhaps an inch long. Holding it up to the light, the White Wolf noted the international bio-hazard symbol adorning the label.

"*Variola nocturnis.* Night Plague. An accomplishment of Russian military bio-engineering." The pride was evident in his voice. "A deadly variant of smallpox, ruthlessly contagious. Each of your men will release this into the water supply of his assigned city. There will be suffering and death on a massive scale."

"Good!"

"We will reduce our enemies to a state of absolute helplessness," said Vetrov. "And then we will utterly crush them."

CHAPTER EIGHT

IT TOOK THEM SOME TIME – several hours of driving and hiking around the desert, examining tire tracks and badgering village elders – but Cody and Hamid finally tracked down the location of Crimson Jihad's basecamp. There was no "a-ha!" moment of revelation where the location was magically revealed. Rather, it was by what *wasn't* said but rather implied, in pursuing enough pathways that petered out into rutted cul-de-sacs that they discovered the place. It was more a process of elimination than outright discovery.

But now they were close, following a steep mountain trail around one of the rocky hills that dotted the forbidding *sahrā*. This region of Syria was sand and more sand, broken occasionally by rocky outcroppings like this hill or the stone valley rumored to be on the other side. Hamid led the way, sure-footed with his daypack and quarter-staff. Cody admired the old Palestinian's stamina. For seventy, he moved like a man half his age.

"You've been here before?" Cody adjusted the fit of

his pack and the cloth bag carrying the M82 all-purpose sniper rifle he had drawn for this mission. With a range of 1,850 meters, the .50-caliber weapon boasted a muzzle velocity of 2,799 feet-per-second. One bullet, accurately fired, could disable an engine block.

"Yes. I enjoy hiking, the outdoors, exploring." Hamid paused and turned back. "I enjoy the country-side. Wherever I am. Is good to put on packsack and walk around. Just to sit and watch Netflix?" He spat in the sand. "This is for stupid people."

"I'm guessing Crimson Jihad has positioned pickets around here somewhere…"

"Not here, Jack Cody." Hamid gestured with his quarter-staff. "You will see. This mountain is barrier, not lookout. Valley on other side is big and difficult enough to control by itself."

"Is the terrain difficult to traverse?"

"A little. But I show you. Never fear!"

Cody chuckled and shook his head as they resumed the journey. He had spent his life knocking around the intelligence world and knew that, despite all eccentrici-ties, men like Hamid were treasured for their ability to improvise and think outside the box. Having overcome his initial apprehensions about the guy, Cody was starting to warm to him.

Nearer the peak, the path flattened, cutting grooves through high stands of rough-hewn rock. Every now and then there would be a break in the stone and Cody could peer into the valley below. It was, as Hamid said, massive and dotted with stone "elephant legs" like Monument Valley back in the States. He got a wide-angle view when the path emerged onto a flat outcropping that jutted out like a knife over the depression.

Hamid took the lead. Crouching low, he crawled to the lip of the outcropping and poked his head up briefly before motioning Cody forward. Cody dropped his daypack, removed the M82 from its bag and slung it on his back. Then he crawled forward to join Hamid.

CHAPTER NINE

Across the valley, Vetrov and the White Wolf moved to the edge of the precipice that overlooked the massed ranks of Crimson Jihad's followers.

More than a thousand had gathered, coming from all points of the region to hear the Great One speak. He had promised to reveal his plans for the next stage of Jihad and so there was excitement among the assembled warriors. To a man, they were desert-dwellers – rural tribesmen, like the White Wolf himself. Although not arranged in rows like western soldiers, they were as one despite their mismatched outfits, headgear and weapons. More than a few went barefoot. Drawn from the great well of Syrian poor, the ranks of Crimson Jihad's followers were men who believed because they had nothing else.

All it took was the White Wolf's stepping forward for a hush to fall over the assembled.

"Warriors! Faithful! Heirs of Saladin!" The White Wolf thrust a clenched fist into the air. "Now the hour has come to cripple and destroy the West! The man you see beside me is the great Russian General Greb Vetrov. It is he who has furnished us with our heart's desire – the weapons of mass destruction needed to finish this holy war! Victory is within reach! *Allahua-akbar!*"

A great cry of joy rose from the warriors. Many raised their fists. Others fired off their weapons in celebration after the desert fashion. At long last, here was the moment they were waiting for – the moment when they would be revenged on the enemies of Islam.

The White Wolf gestured for silence before continuing.

"With this, our movement reaches a new phase! A phase that would have been impossible to achieve without your faithfulness! Without your dedication! Without your prayers! Now that moment has been reached! And it is time to say…goodbye!"

Looks of puzzlement crossed the faces of one thousand jihadis simultaneously.

"Not all of you will be coming with me on this mission. In fact, the vast majority of you will not! This is something that requires a new type of warrior! Do I accuse anyone of cowardice or shirking? Far from it! You were the best, the dearest, the most dedicated and bold of Islam's warriors! But now your fight is done."

A strange droning sound filled the air.

"I send you to your reward with gratitude and love."

With these words, the White Wolf closed his remarks. A moment later, two Russian combat helicopters appeared in the skies above.

———

CODY STARTED when he saw them. He had been drawing a bead on Vetrov, whose figure was obscured by the animated form of the White Wolf and was just about to squeeze off when a blur crossed his viewfinder and the helicopters appeared.

"Russian choppers! You see, Jack Cody?"

"I see." Cody looked up from the viewfinder and frowned. "What the hell is the White Wolf doing?"

Those were the last words he would speak for a while.

———

THE FIRST HELICOPTER unleashed a howling barrage of missile fire. The weapons streaked into the valley below, detonating among the assembled warriors in great gusts of flame. Explosions rocked the ground. The second chopper swung around and conducted a strafing run, its Yak Gatling gun chattering to life and shredding the men who ran, desperately seeking cover among the rocks. But what little there was soon became dust under the power of computer-guided weapons fire.

Vetrov and the White Wolf surveyed the slaughter impassively from the valley's edge. Both wore the same expression of calm indifference, watching the automated killing with all the enthusiasm one might muster watching a car commercial on television. This was war. Men were expendable. To win victories sacrifices must be made. This was understood between them without a word being spoken.

The butchery, the betrayal and immorality of their action?

Well, in life there are winners…and losers.

The slaughter continued.

Everything happened so fast. One minute Cody was grappling the M82 from its position on the rocky outcropping, the next he was twisting to run. Hamid, a little further ahead, had paused, waving for Cody to hurry up, pour on the speed, get clear. And then the world crashed in on him.

The missile streaked across the valley, aiming for the furthermost jihadis – the ones standing at the valley's edge – when it missed and slammed into the rock wall below Cody's position. It detonated, vaporizing the cliff's edge and setting rocks above it to tumble. Cody ran through a shower of grit, then slate chunks. It was finally a boulder the size of a soccer ball that bounced off his left shoulder and put his lights out.

Up the path, Hamid turned.

Cody!

Instantly, he was sprinting back and falling to his knees beside the half-buried man. Cody lay face-down, covered in rubble to the waist. Hamid grasped the nearest chunk and lifted it away. Then he was digging furiously, his hands paddling dirt one moment, claw-grasping rocks the next. He dug on, ignoring the pain of the cuts and broken nails. He dug with the desperation of a man determined to save a life, for he was. All around them, the violence and carnage continued to churn. He would bring Cody to safety, regardless of the risk to his own. For this he was prepared to sacrifice his life. The laws of desert hospitality demanded no less.

———

In a high geosynchronous orbit three hundred miles above, close attention was being paid to the drama unfolding below.

A lens – one about the size of a regulation USSBA softball – twisted and rotated within its steel lid, focus dilating until it picked out the ant-crawl of activity unfolding in the valley. The optics of the Justice-SAT-142 satellite were not Keyhole-comparable, but came about as close as a civilian spacecraft could to the level of orbital surveillance enjoyed by the likes of Pentagon and CIA. The optics could not read the license plate of a car or label on the pack of cigarettes. But it was more than equal to the task of picking out known persons of interest.

The image from the satellite was beamed across a secure encrypted network and then downloaded to a server hub in the Order of World Harmony, where it was viewed onscreen in the office of Windy Duke, personal assistant to Thelma Justice.

"It does appear to be Jack Cody," he said. She was speaking into the audio-phone, with a direct connection to the Order's affiliate in Jordan. "I want you to see who we have in the region that is available to work this. We need eyes on and guns on the ground. Vetrov is under a comms blackout just now. We'll alert him in another…" She squinted at her desk clock. "Thirteen minutes. They should be done disposing of the White Wolf's followers by then. Follow up with me on the hour."

She clicked off and returned her attention to the flatscreen monitor.

It seemed Cody's companion had made headway. The tiny dark figure of the Palestinian operative was bent over and pulling the inert figure of Cody out to the rubble, and closer to safety. Windy Duke hit the control toggle on the satellite panel to zoom closer.

The Palestinian had Cody by the shoulders and was dragging him backwards out of the debris. He had made admirable progress. Now a hundred yards out he paused and bent, grasping and lifting Cody over his shoulder, securing him in a fireman's carry and then moving swiftly down the path away from the slaughter. At that moment, the lens fuzzed out and the image pixelated.

Windy Duke cursed. She had lost them.

CHAPTER TEN

Alone, Aisha walked the streets of Paris, her features concealed behind a scarf, her senses alert to danger.

A night and day had passed since she had killed the man in the public *pissoir*. She had remained on the move, pausing only now and then to rest her legs over a coffee in a fast-food joint, or stretch her limbs and wash up for a luxurious half-hour in a library washroom. Everything was a jumbled blur. And she knew she had to get off the street.

Her brother, Achmed, had tried catching her. Following the instructions of their dying father, the sheikh, he had come after her with a group of his men, only to face the wrath of Cody and the Vatican team that sought her. At the heart of all of it was the Tablet. She now wished she had never encountered the thing.

In the end, she thought, *it all comes down to belief, and what that belief can inspire people to do on its behalf.*

She was tired of intrigues, tired of manipulations. She was hungry for truth.

The Relic had at first promised something like truth.

Known by many names, it was a clay tablet upon which had been recorded the details of a visit by a man named Yeshua to a community to desert-dwelling rabbis living outside Jerusalem in 1 AD. The narrative recounted a sermon by this 'Jesus' containing an alternate version of the Book of Genesis as well as surprising details about Yeshua and his family.

Of course, the scholars who had vied with each other for possession of the Relic throughout history surmised this recounted a story of the New Testament figure of Jesus. As a Muslim, Aisha was perhaps more open to this idea than any Christian invested in the notion of Biblical inerrancy. Islam itself devotes a substantive share of its literature to Jesus of Nazareth – a different sort of Jesus from the one in the Bible, but nevertheless claiming historical parallel. A relic dating from the earliest days of the First Century purporting to be about Christ, providing alternate accounts of Creation and the family lineage of the Savior. It was perhaps of no surprise that such a treasure might prove controversial – controversial enough to kill for.

Aisha was now the custodian of the Relic. It was being kept safe in a location that only she knew. She believed that made it her responsibility to share its existence with those most likely to use it for the common good of all.

The Roman Catholic church had already tried to kill her for it. Foreign agents likewise pursued the Relic. Aisha had originally determined to share it with Thelma Justice, the women's empowerment and self-help guru. That plan had become knocked off-course when her brother's men had come into conflict with the security staff at the Thelma Justice event in DC. Aisha had been convinced by a CIA agent named Sara Durell to trust her. Sara Durell and Jack Cody had protected her, had kept their word and had not tried to coerce or influence her regarding the Relic in any way whatsoever.

But that didn't mean they – or the government for which they worked – wouldn't try to influence her regarding the Relic at some point in the future.

She had to be sure.

So she had disappeared. After their last operation, in which Cody and Sara had taken down a black-market nuclear weapons transaction, once she was sure they were safe, she left their protection. In point of fact, she had done so suspecting they would not approve. But…

She had to be sure.

The Relic was too important, its potential significance way too powerful to simply *entrust* it to someone on the basis of her own opinion. The text about the desert rabbi who told the alternate story of Creation (for, indeed, if it really *was* Him, He'd have been present at the Event) would have to be shared with someone who had the spiritual as well as the political understanding.

The Church had tried to kill her.

Cody and Sara worked for the American government.

Her brother was a creature of politics and power.

What she needed was a spiritual advisor. And who better than Thelma Justice?

SARA DURELL STALKED Aisha through the streets of Paris. Up and down the boulevards, head bowed, eyes down on the tracker in her hand, she marched past shops, hotels, apartment buildings, tourist sites. She moved with the dogged grace of a she-wolf. The streets

unwound beneath her heels, the tracker signal occasionally hiccupping on electrostatic interference, dead spots,
Wi-Fi traffic jams. Particularly irritating was the signal's
habit of deviating between 'real time' and past tense.
Some moments, she would see the glowing dot of the
tracker in motion and, at others, the signal remaining
still for long periods of time before suddenly becoming
jarred to a whole new section of the map.

Last night, she had been sure she was onto the girl. A
particularly strong signal was emanating from Montmartre. Sara had hurried there, arriving to find a public
washroom roped off and guarded by police. She watched
as paramedics carried out a body on a stretcher. She
noted the blood, the locale and the height of the victim.
Too tall to be Aisha. But perhaps someone she had been
forced to kill in self-defense?

She kept on.

The tangled streets spiraled out ahead, the grime of
old Paris meeting the grime and stainless steel of new
Paris. The signal stuck at one place that turned out to be
a fast-food restaurant. Sara could imagine Aisha stopping
in for a quick bite to eat before resuming her trek...

Where?

Sara had her ideas.

The signal was moving again, now stopped, now
moving again. It gummed up at a branch of the library –
a building large enough to obtain its own schematic on
the tracker's screen. The glowing bead that had been
Aisha lingered in a washroom. Sara stood in the echoing
lavatory, imagining Aisha freshening up before resuming
her journey.

She was about to exit when a crowd of people
standing around a flatscreen image projecting the news
caught her attention. She drifted over.

There on-screen: the image of the public lavatory from earlier today, of police carrying out a body on a stretcher.

"...he was found dead in the women's washroom!" Sara heard one man exclaim.

"It was probably some faggot who got robbed while having his *pizou* sucked," joked another.

The screen cleared, cutting to a news broadcaster. Behind her, an image from CCTV appeared, eventually enlarged to fill the screen.

Aisha.

There could be no doubt about it. Although the face was covered with a scarf, Sara recognized the clothes, the physique and the messenger bag in which had been sewn the tracking device she now followed. A word crawl on-screen urged viewers to call police if they had any information on the whereabouts of this person, suspected of murder.

So the police were after her now.

Sara hurried to the library door. She had no time to waste.

CHAPTER ELEVEN

CODY SWAM from unconsciousness toward wakefulness. It was a confusing swim, buoyed in a blur of lights, voices and abrupt changes in volume. His semi-consciousness was a jumble of stimuli, finally jarring him awake in a small, windowless room of clay daubed walls. There was relative silence all around.

A barefoot woman entered through a narrow wooden doorway, grasping the scarf around her neck and pulling it to her face when she saw he was awake. Cody scarcely got a look at her, but the eyes were visible, and he detected a devilish sense of humor there that reminded him of ...

"*Ha – MIIID!*" She was laughing out loud and stumbling slightly, grasping the veil modestly to her face while steadying herself with the other. She had short-nails and clever, blunt fingers. Her bare feet were broad, suggesting that she had had children. When Hamid Hassan poked his head in the doorway, Cody saw the resemblance immediately.

"Cody! Man!" The Palestinian rushed in and dropped to his knees beside Cody's bed. "Hamid thought you were dead, man. Finished. Thank Allah you came back."

Cody smiled, reached out and gripped Hamid's forearms. He squeezed and tested the muscles in his back and legs. Everything seemed to be in working order. "Where am I?"

"At the house of my brother-in-law, Feti. He's a Turk. My sister Miriam marry him and they move to western Syria, near Jordanian border. Cody. Somehow, government knows you are here. Alert has been issued – your name, your face, all over the news. You rest and then we get you out of country, across border into Jordan. Feti and Miriam help."

This was an awful lot to absorb, but Cody took it in, processed it and nodded. Miriam and Feti were, so far as he could tell, civilian bystanders who were nonetheless willing to step up and help a stranger in need, despite any possible danger to themselves. Cody had seen it many times before. It strengthened his belief in people and his determination to fight on their behalf.

"Thank you, Miriam and Feti," he said. As he did, Feti, a tall mustachioed man, stepped into the room, wrapped an arm protectively around his wife and grinned at Cody, waving a thumbs up.

The good people of this world, Cody thought, *far outweigh the bad.*

He allowed that thought to linger before he drifted off again.

Cody LIMPED out of the bedroom shortly after dawn to find Feti sitting on a wooden bench, fiddling with a transistor radio. He looked up, grin flashing beneath his mustache as he gave Cody a thumbs up. Cody smiled, waved back and limped outside. There was a small courtyard attached to Miriam and Feti's house. Cody saw a low wooden bench similar to Feti's by the wall to his left. He limped over and sat. And when he did, his mind was blown.

A low mud wall enclosed the courtyard. To Cody's right was a tall sign bearing the familiar logo of Colonel Saunders with red Arabic lettering where 'KFC' should be. The sign, elevated on a black iron pole, was obviously a billboard of some type. It inhabited a skyscape dotted with aerials and satellite dishes.

To Cody's left was an open gate. Beyond it lay desert scrub where goats fed and a lone boy in robes guided a young camel by the rope around its neck. Beyond them lay the interminable wastes of western Syria.

I must be in some kind of suburb, Cody thought. The notion of 'suburban Syria' was an odd one, but Cody accepted that whatever little 'ville Hamid's sister and brother-in-law had chosen was on the line of civilization between old and modern Syria. *This is likely where the tribe meets the city, where jihad meets McWorld...*

Hamid, relaxed into the informality of his family setting, came out and joined Cody, shirtless and wearing flip-flops. He sat down besides Cody and began pulling apart an orange.

"*Salaam aleikum,* brother Cody. By God's grace, you live." He handed over a section of orange. "It was by merest providence I turned in time to see. I am grateful to Feti and Miriam. They take a risk having us here."

"I know it." Cody stretched. "The sooner we go, the better."

"You will leave tonight." Hamid Hassan squinted up at the sky. "Sunset in about twelve hours. Stay awake now. Sleep when the sun is highest. Wake at dusk. My brothers will be here." He patted Cody's knee.

"Brothers?"

Hamid nodded. "Bedouin. They are beautiful men. True men. Warriors of the old way. Syrians don't like Bedouin under current government. Because Bedouin don't participate in census, do military service, pay taxes… They live the traditional way. By their wits. In tents. In desert. Use their camels go from here to there. Bedou? Hurt *nobody.* They drift back and forth across the border between Jordan and Syria like it don't exist. You drift with them tonight. Jordan is CIA control station, with Backchannel operative. I let him know you come."

"Hamid, I don't know what to say."

"Go get White Wolf. Kill son-of-a-bitch. Help my nation to heal. Too many wolves in the Middle East nowadays, Jack Cody. We need more diplomats."

———

CODY DID AS HAMID SUGGESTED. He ate a delicious meal prepared by Miriam, and served by both Miriam and Feti, with much formality, fussing and thumbs-upping. Then Cody relaxed into a joyful and effortless slumber that brought him blissful oblivion.

He awakened, sharp, fresh and eager to move.

He got out of bed, put on his tactical pants and hoodie, pulled on his tac boots and stuffed his sidearms, knives and various munitions away before stepping out to the courtyard and an unbelievable sight.

Just beyond the gate out in the scrub behind Feti and Mariam's house, a dozen camels kitted out in long-range desert riding gear were kneeling at rest. And their Bedouin riders, festooned with rifles and long-swords, paced restlessly, awaiting him. Cody moved forward to meet his official escort into Jordan.

CHAPTER TWELVE

JUST FIVE METERS outside the gate to the courtyard and they were in open desert. Hamid and Feti approached the headman of the group and spoke with him briefly in Arabic. Then Hamid turned and gestured for Cody to approach.

"Jack Cody, meet Reza ibn-Melik," said Hamid. "He is the patriarch of his clan and leads this group of raiders. His ancestral homelands are across the border in Jordan. Ibn-Melik and his people do not recognize the border, or the authority of the Syrian government. I have explained that you are an enemy of the government."

Hamid followed this up with a brief statement in Arabic to the headman. Ibn-Melik listened impassively, examining Cody with about the same amount of interest one might reserve for an interesting cloud formation or household pet. When Hamid finished, ibn-Melik turned and spoke sharply to the men in their tribal dialect. They approached their camels and began preparing them for departure. One of the younger men of the group, perhaps all of nineteen, stepped forward and acknowledged Cody with a nod.

"This is Abdul, Reza's grandson. You will ride with him." Hamid extended a hand. "God bless you, Jack Cody. Good luck."

They shook. Abdul stepped forward and extended his hand awkwardly in the unfamiliar gesture of a western handshake and pumped Cody's hand twice. He spoke to Hamid and turned to Cody, waiting for the translation.

"Abdul says not to worry." Hassan smiled. "You are under his protection. Your safety and comfort are his responsibility. He will see to it that you are well cared for."

"Please thank him for me," said Cody.

Hassan did. Abdul listened to the exchange, nodded and patted Cody on the shoulder. Then he grinned, exposing several chipped teeth, and gestured for Cody to follow him. They approached one of the kneeling camels.

The beast swung its massive head toward them, examining Cody skeptically. He got the sense that the camel was a quick-tempered beast, not easily impressed. He noted how Abdul spoke to it in a harsh, clipped tone. *Showing it who's boss,* Cody thought. He knew it was important to show horses who was in charge. Given the size and violent potential of these great desert beasts, he guessed similar rules applied.

In amongst the great and ponderous load balanced on the beast's back, the camel itself had two small wooden seats affixed there. The fragile wooden structure reminded Cody of a child's car seat, but as he settled himself, he found it roomy and surprisingly comfortable.

"Murih?" Abdul asked, then he laughed with a kind of good-humored teasing that made Cody instantly warm to him. He could tell Abdul was the junior partner

of the group, eager to prove himself to the older men. Based on the looks of approval Abdul received from them, he did not have much left to prove. Cody felt sure he was in good hands.

With a command from ibn-Melik, the camels rose as one. Following the headman in single file, they began to hike into the desert. The beasts moved at what felt to Cody like a nice, leisurely pace, but their long strides meant they covered a lot of ground with relatively few steps. After what felt like only a minute or two, he looked back and was surprised to see the distant silhouette of Feti throwing him one last thumb's up before they topped a rise and the lights of the house and the city itself became lost from view.

Being out on the ocean at night was the closest analogue to the journey as Cody experienced it. The desert became pitch black, or so it seemed, for a half-hour or so. But soon Cody's eyes adjusted to the lack of urban light pollution, and he began to discern features of terrain. Out here in the deep night, a sliver of moon, the light it reflected from clouds and the twinkle of stars were enough to illuminate the land. After about an hour, Cody heard traffic sounds.

They topped a rise and looked down on a stretch of narrow highway. A gas station hugged the shoulder of the road on the opposite side, light spilling from its neon sign onto the terrain. Ibn-Melik pointed to the gas pumps, waved his hands and spoke a brief monologue to the group. Whatever he was saying, it didn't sound terribly complimentary. When he was done, he led the way down the dune and across the highway to the other side. As the last camel driver slipped into the shadows behind the gas station with the group, a police car pulled off the road into the service station. A lone cop got out holding a sheet of paper in his hands and went inside. He wasn't in there long before he emerged, got back into his car and sped away.

"Abdul," said ibn-Melik. When the young man looked over, the elder jerked his chin toward the service station.

Abdul eased his camel into the kneeling position, slipped off and strode out of the shadows into the light from the service station. He went inside. Two minutes later, he emerged, approached the group and produced a rolled-up page from his sleeve, which he handed to ibn-Melik. The old man unrolled the page, studied it and then laughed, holding the paper aloft. The group laughed with him. Then he urged his camel to go stand by Abdul's as it rose to a standing position.

"*Y'ala,*" he said, handing the paper to Cody. Cody accepted it with a nod of thanks and unraveled it. Staring back at him was a grainy reproduction of his own face in a fuzzy photocopy. He widened his eyes and turned to ibn-Melik.

The Bedouin elder was grinning broadly. Somehow, this wanted poster proved Cody's bona-fides to ibn-Melik's satisfaction.

"*Jeck Koh-dee,*" said the old man. His eyes held Cody's and he nodded meaningfully. Cody knew that his being a wanted man cemented his acceptance among the Bedouin. And that was just fine with him.

As one, the camel train turned and ventured deeper into the desert.

CHAPTER THIRTEEN

THE WHITE WOLF pitched his camp a quarter mile from the resort. This far from the capital, he could likely have entered the compound as a guest's visitor with minimal risk, but when he imagined doing such a thing, he felt a visceral disgust. He despised hotels, resorts and the tourist industry in general. They brought the pollution of infidels to the sacred desert. The White Wolf shuddered in revulsion at the thought of the alcohol, bare flesh and immorality abounding beyond those stucco walls. He was just as happy to pitch his tent here with a few loyal bodyguards and meet his guests on his home turf of the desert.

A black SUV stopped on the dirt road leading to the gated resort and two passengers alighted, a man and a woman. A lone guard carrying a Kalashnikov shadowed them at a distance. The White Wolf recognized his confederate Vetrov and felt a shimmer of discomfort seeing the woman by his side.

That must be Thelma Justice, he thought. Although not one to own a television or surf the internet, he was nevertheless aware of her position as a sort of spiritual advisor to the world's women. *Heretic,* he thought. Anyone claiming to be 'spiritual' who did not preach Q'uran was automatically an imposter in the White Wolf's eyes.

But wars required alliances. His men had engaged in ad hoc alliances with groups as far-flung as al-Qaeda, Hezbollah and Red September. Even with such brothers, there had been tensions. He expected worse with Thelma Justice. But...

The enemy of my enemy is my friend, he reminded himself, stepping from his tent with a smile.

"Hello, my friend!" Vetrov gave a cheery wave. The White Wolf noted how the Russian had linked arms with the woman. Perhaps they were lovers. The White Wolf thought that might explain the erratic nature of Vetrov's decision making.

"*Salaam aleikum,*" said the White Wolf solemnly. Ordinarily, he would have spoken only to the man, but circumstances dictated that he treat the woman Thelma Justice like an equal partner. He found the experience unnatural, grating. But for the glory of the Prophet, he was prepared to endure any indignity. Even this.

He conducted them into his tent, where one of his warriors served them almond cakes and mint tea in tiny cups. The White Wolf watched Thelma Justice surreptitiously as she sat and attended to the food and her role as guest in the Imam's tent. Vetrov must have briefed her, for she behaved with a combination of confidence and humility the White Wolf found pleasing.

"And so," Vetrov finished his tea and set down his glass to be refilled, "it is my pleasure to introduce the woman who will assist your warriors in infiltrating the enemy's nations and cities. Allow me to present Ms. Thelma Justice."

The White Wolf nodded to Thelma Justice, who beamed a bright smile but did not offer her hand. Aware that she was probably accustomed to doing so with western men, he appreciated her restraint and decorum.

"Your organization is made up of women, correct?" the White Wolf's tone was clinical, matter-of-fact.

"It *is*." Thelma Justice caught her own "so what?" tone and modified it. "Yes. It is."

"My men will not take orders from women. You must understand this." The White Wolf nodded, agreeing with himself. "When dealing with my men, the women must be aware of their place. They must assist. They must support. And then they must stand aside."

Thelma Justice seemed on the point of arguing when Vetrov interposed smoothly.

"Ms. Justice and her organization you will find very professional. Very effective."

"And they will do what?"

Vetrov looked to Thelma and nodded.

"We have made arrangements to lease a dozen private aircraft," she said. "They will fly in and out of Damascus under cover as a commercial courier. We've modified the craft with corporate logos, false manifests, the works. Each of your men will be given a jumpsuit with the false carrier's logo on the breast pocket. They will show up at the airport, make their way to the commercial terminal. They will not be stopped from boarding the aircraft as they will appear to be employees. The planes have trans-oceanic range. Each flight will be capable of taking your men to their final destinations in Europe and the Americas."

"Once they arrive—"

"Once they arrive," said the White Wolf, interrupting Vetrov, "they will require no assistance. Provided they have the weapons you promise, they will release it in the water supply. The horror will begin."

"It will." Vetrov's words contained a note of satisfaction.

"But you say this is only opening act." The White Wolf narrowed his eyes. "You speak of a great hammer from on high. Speak to me about this."

Vetrov and Thelma looked at each other. Some wordless communication passed between them.

"We have made a friend." Vetrov paused. "Ms. Justice's organization has a strategic advantage. If she can get to a man's wife, the wife in turn can get to the man."

"So your organization has turned someone important." The White Wolf folded his arms, appraising her with cool skepticism. "Who?"

"An individual very highly placed in the United States military infrastructure."

The White Wolf raised his eyebrows. This had been unexpected. "You intend to turn the weapons of our oppressors against them?"

Vetrov nodded.

"What weapons?"

"You shall see, my friend," Vetrov promised. "You shall see, and I can promise you that you will not be disappointed."

"You realize," said Thelma Justice, "there is a very good chance your men will die delivering the contagion."

"This is of no consequence." The White Wolf flapped a hand. "It does not matter how many martyrs die. What matters is how many of the enemy are killed."

CHAPTER FOURTEEN

AISHA KEPT her head down and continued moving, aware now that the police were after her. She had seen the television broadcasts with the still photos from the CCTV feed – her in a panicked blur, running from the *pissoir* where she'd killed that man. Ducking into a laundromat had allowed her to steal some clothing to alter her appearance but she still had the same shoes and messenger bag and was still one girl wandering by herself through the streets of Paris. Obvious. Vulnerable. Alone.

So she kept moving. Public buildings only – libraries, museums, community centers. She would enter circumspectly, eyes down, and find a place to sit and commune with her laptop. She tried never to remain for longer than an hour or two. Sometimes this strategy paid dividends. Sometimes it did not.

Being cautious at the bus station had enabled her to retreat there at nightfall and gain access to a private washroom set aside for parents with infants. She had slipped in without anyone noticing and enjoyed a glorious five hours of privacy during which time she had washed her socks and underwear and recharged her laptop. She even managed to catnap for a few hours. She emerged just as dawn was etching the eastern sky, not even eliciting a glance of curiosity from the janitor mopping the platform. A friendly ticket agent had wished her *bonjour* and held open the door as she exited.

The library, on the other hand, had proven a close shave. She had not even known that public libraries had security guards these days, but it came as no surprise. The questionable figures she had seen lurking around the entrances, sheltering from the rain in doorways, setting up in the quiet areas of the stacks with their backpacks and garbage bags stuffed with possessions were *bommes* – the street people of Paris. Some came in to sleep, others to deal drugs. It was with a start that she realized: she was now one of them.

The guard on duty this day was a younger man, likely a prospect for the police or military. Stiff necked, his uniform pressed, and his skull shaved to a brush cut, he was more attentive and engaged than the average guard. He took note of Aisha while patrolling the second floor, so she moved to the third. When his rounds took him there, he slowed as he passed her, eyes flicking that quick "up-and-down" glance cops and guards give persons of interest. In that moment, she realized that moving had sparked his notice. She should have stayed put.

She packed up and left. After a few hours spent lingering in an open-air market and the train station, she returned. She was just starting to get comfortable on a couch by the reference desk when she saw the guard again. It was the same sharp-eyed, brush-cut kid she'd seen earlier. He perked up and did a close walk-by of her position. *I remember you from earlier,* his eyes said.

She began immediately stowing her stuff. The laptop and power cord went into the messenger bag, and it was over her shoulder while he was still switching direction to come speak to her. She plunged down a row of books that ended at a steel fire door. She pushed her way through, descended the stairs and ended up standing among a trio of other young homeless.

"Is the guard coming?" one asked as the fire door crashed open on the landing above and the guard's footsteps could be heard descending. As one, they fled through the exit and into the rain, laughing. Aisha, having no reason to either trust or distrust them, ran alongside, laughing too. It felt good to be part of a group again.

A few blocks later they paused, certain they were not being pursued. The four of them came to rest below the marquee of an abandoned theatre. The posters up in their glass display cases were for films that were years out of date. One of the boys pulled out a pack of cigarettes and began passing it around.

"That was close, hey? Here, here … have a Gitanes. Hey! Only one! *Salaud!* I got a lighter. Just a sec. Hey." He paused at Aisha's refusal. "What's the matter? New to the streets, are you? Refusing a free gift?"

"I don't smoke." Aisha said it with a smile, hoping to soften the refusal. But she could tell that wouldn't work.

"Little princess is health conscious," said the other girl in the group.

Aisha tried smiling again to hide her discomfort but only succeeded in making it more obvious. This occasioned more laughter from the group, and a hard look from the boy who had offered her a cigarette.

"I'm Jean," he told her. "The other one? He's Jean,

too. But we call him 'Ti Jean. That means 'Little John'. The girl is Michelle."

"Aisha." She pointed to herself and inclined her head in greeting.

"Aisha, we'll take your bag. Give us the bag and laptop and we'll let you walk away. If not, we'll put you in the hospital. Got it?"

Aisha's good feelings logjammed on a horrified lump in her solar plexus. *We'll take...?* She was still processing these words when 'Ti Jean, still laughing, reached for the bag. His laugh ended when her punch connected with his mouth. Then they were on her.

Jean managed to grab a handful of her hair and punch her in the gut. She folded but rabbit-punched between his legs. Michelle's kick connected with her eye, blinding her. Then suddenly *they* were shouting, scattering and a hard-voiced woman was shouting in French. Aisha rolled to her knees.

The woman who stood there wore a uniform – not Paris police. Aisha recognized it from Moscow, when she had visited Thelma Justice's Russian headquarters. The woman looked down on Aisha with concern. "I am Julie Bedard, chief of security for the Order of World Harmony. Here. Let me help you."

CHAPTER FIFTEEN

"MR. PRESIDENT?" The Secret Service agent hovered in the doorway of the White House gym. "Mr. Parnell is outside, sir."

"Send him in."

President Martin Harwood completed his twenty-fifth inclined sit-up, fingers laced behind his neck, grunting with effort as he brought elbows to knees then lay back. His breathing was labored, but not heavy. In his T-shirt and track pants, he cut an impressive figure for his sixty-odd years. Although leader of the Free World, he was adamant that a period of exercise be worked into his schedule. Such periods tended to occur between four and five AM, as it now did.

Jared Parnell entered the room, self-conscious in his business attire, his hair slightly ruffled, the stink of his cherrywood vape pen clinging to him like a bad case of body odor. The president caught whiff of it at twenty paces and wrinkled his nose.

"Christ, Parnell. You still sucking on that vape pen?"

"Never on the White House grounds, Mr. President."

"Good." Harwood rose from the incline bench, grabbed a towel and began wiping the sweat from his forehead and neck. "Thank you for coming at this early hour. I have a full day ahead. The Japanese prime minister arrives for a state visit in three hours, but I wanted to get an update on CIA's efforts to locate General Vetrov."

"Yes, sir." Parnell produced his Android phone and began thumbing through his notebook app. "Per your permission, sir, we sent CIA special operations group to Monte Carlo to follow up on the stolen nukes. I am please to report their mission was one hundred per cent successful. We retrieved the missing Russian suitcase nukes."

"So the director said." The president grabbed a bottle of water from a nearby shelf. "But there were a couple of things he mentioned that I didn't understand."

"I'll do my best to clear up your questions, sir."

"Okay." Harwood sipped, toyed with his bottle and then sipped again before speaking. "He mentioned an excavation of some kind. Apparently, your guys contacted French intelligence about sourcing them a couple of front-end loaders?"

"Um." Parnell's finger danced above the Android screen. "Uh, yes, sir. Our allies in Paris were—"

"I received a phone call from the President of France yesterday." Harwood frowned. "He was pretty pissed off. Apparently, he had his team do a follow up sweep of the, ah, 'excavation' site. With a Geiger counter."

"Oh…"

"Yeah." The president took a seat on the bench. "Jared…why did you need construction machinery?"

"Well, sir. The, ah, nukes were located *in situ* on an

estate owned by Thelma Justice. We have reason to believe she is now working with Vetrov."

"Thelma Justice. Okay. I'll have our people look into it."

"We have actually obtained some surveillance photos of the two of them together. Just came in—"

"Parnell…"

"…from our agents in Marseilles. Apparently, they—"

"The construction equipment."

"The construction equipment! Right!" His eyes went back to the phone. "So the estate had undergone some sort of counterintelligence action."

"You mean somebody showed up and trashed the place before you got there."

"We, um, *did* find it to be in some disarray, yes, sir."

"How *much* disarray?"

"Ah… Well, there was evidence of gunfire. Some explosions. And the, ah, house itself was… Well…"

"Out with it!"

"It was a pile of rubble." Parnell pocketed his Android and shrugged. "It was a large house. A mansion. Thousands of square feet."

"Reduced to rubble. Tell me, Jared. What would it take to do something like that?"

"Well, it could have been any number of explosive devices, sir…"

"Don't mess with me, son." Harwood narrowed his eyes at the CIA flunkey. "You remember I *do* have a military background…"

"Yes, sir. Thank you for that service, by the way."

"And I happen to know that large buildings – particularly large, expensively-built ones – don't just collapse became some asshole chucks a Molotov cocktail through a window. It takes a good deal more than that to collapse a façade, supporting beams and upper floors. Now, if I were going to do something like that, I'd probably use a helicopter."

"I see. Yes, sir."

"Preferably one armed with the latest, greatest array of anti-personnel and anti-tank weaponry available. It seems that just such a chopper was found abandoned on a building site in Monte Carlo. French intelligence went over it with a fine-tooth comb."

"Yes, sir?"

"It was a modified Russian combat helicopter. It had a phalanx of air-to-ground missiles, a Gatling gun and various other goodies of the type used to demolish the house."

"Oh?"

"Oh, yes." Harwood sighed. "I'm going to put a scenario to you, Parnell. Tell me what you think."

"Sure thing, sir."

"See, I'm thinking that a couple of our agents – possibly agents that are currently off-the grid, so to speak – managed to intercept the Russians arranging transfer of the nukes. I'm thinking these agents – who are, after all, skilled enough to evade the American, Russian and British intelligence efforts to locate them – managed to compromise the transfer. Then they hijacked the chopper, homed in on the location of the nukes and leveled the place."

"That's – wow. Rather, uh, fanciful...?"

"Really? When we have agents like Jack Cody at large and off the grid just now? Not to mention Sara Durell, who is a trained combat helicopter pilot? Both of whom were recently in Monte Carlo?"

"Um…"

"See, I'm thinking that's likely what happened." The president smiled. "*They* recovered the nukes. You, on the other hand, deployed the most costly special operations group in the US arsenal to act as a glorified courier mission and clean-up crew for our French allies."

"Well, sir. In all fairness. We *did* get the nukes back…"

"Bullshit. Jack Cody and Sara Durell got them back. You and your boys just picked up the loose ends. Here." He handed Parnell a slip of paper. "Make yourself useful. See if you can locate that guy."

Parnell read the paper. "Hamid Hassan, sir?"

"Palestinian. Former Mossad agent now living in Syria. He's apparently the last guy to see Cody. Or, at least, that's what my sources tell me. Track him down. Find out where Cody went. If it's not too much trouble."

"Uh, no sir. No, sir. Not at all."

"Thank you." The president slung the towel over his shoulder and grabbed up the water bottle. "Now if you'll excuse me. I have a tuxedo fitting and a lesson on conversational Japanese to attend before our state visit."

"Yes, sir. Thank you, Mr. President."

Parnell departed in a hurry, desperate to take a pull off his vape pen.

CHAPTER SIXTEEN

THE CAMEL TRAIN'S trek through the Syrian desert continued. Cody had deployed into desert terrain before, but this was his first long-term exposure to the environment. He was surprised by how varied the weather and terrain became along the way. Rather than the flat sands portrayed in classic Hollywood movies, the desert was a region of varied character, becoming colder and hotter, or more wooded or sparse depending on the altitude one traveled. When they paused to make camp or bivouac, ibn-Melik's men inevitably chose the lowlands. Cody could see why. The sandier desert was riddled with little valleys and depressions perfect for literally 'lying low'.

They were not alone. A few times on the trail, the headman had called a halt and pointed skyward. The rest would peer up from their camels. Inevitably, a plane would materialize flying high above, unnoticed by all save he. Cody surmised they were likely border patrol flights, searching for smugglers or insurgents. The Bedouin train would likely be noticed and logged but

Cody knew his presence among them would not. Hamid Hassan's instincts had been good.

One thing Hollywood got right, Cody thought, *were the tents.*

The group did deploy tents for the overnight bivouacs and, occasionally, during their daylight rest stops. The tents were stoutly-made examples of folk craftsmanship – attractive, utilitarian and serviceable. Cody noted how, when they wanted to, these same tents could be collapsed and partially covered with sand, providing a sort of natural hunter's blind. The Bedouin could put out their tents this way and vanish into the sand, the only trace of them being the camels hobbled nearby.

The tents had been so arrayed when the soldiers struck.

Perhaps it had been that plane ibn-Melik had spotted. Or perhaps it was just a random crackdown. But the roar of Jeep engines split the dusk and the Bedouins came to alert. First among them was ibn-Melik. He emerged from his tent, disheveled and barefoot from a nap, nevertheless alert. His loose hair framing his face, he looked every inch the desert lion as he cried to his men, punching his rifle aloft as he rallied them. Then the first Jeep plunged over the edge of the depression, barreling straight toward him.

Ibn-Melik remained calm. He steadied his stance, threw his rifle to his shoulder and began firing round after round through the windshield. The Bedouin chieftain did not flinch as the vehicle wobbled off course, coming within bare inches of him as it careened toward the edge of a *wadi* before flipping over and bursting into flames. Ibn-Melik nodded that this was good, spat and turned to face the next Jeep.

Abdul stumbled up to Cody, reached into his belt and withdrew a revolver. He said something in Arabic, then thrust the weapon into Cody's hands. Cody thanked him and gave the thing a quick scan. *You've got to be kidding me,* he thought. The clumsy old firearm was a Webley, the sort of thing British soldiers in pith helmets wore back when they were still trying to colonize Africa. But it was loaded, and the enemy was closing in, so he extended his arm and squeezed the trigger.

BLAM-O! The thing went off like a small cannon in his fist, shredding a Jeep driver's skull and causing his vehicle to tumble and crash.

"Jeck Codee!" Ibn-Melik grinned and thrust a fist aloft.

The Syrians were pouring into the area – three more Jeeps, a standing rear gunner operating a mounted sixty-cal. in each. He watched as a hail of bullets skidded across a dune, startling the nearby camels. He saw at once that a half-dozen of the beasts were hobbled – sitting ducks for the bobbing and weaving Jeeps. That's when he also saw Abdul, sprinting over to free them. One of the Jeeps, noting this, turned and bore down on the boy.

Cody spun and went after it, arm extended, the Webley blazing bullets. Two shredded the front tire and the Jeep sank nose-first into the sand. The sixty-cal. in back jammed.

He leapt onto the hood, got a foot on top of the windshield and launched himself over the driver at the machine-gunner. The man stumbled back, shocked at the frontal assault. Cody landed on the guy and began clubbing him with the empty Webley.

The driver recovered his shock, twisted and began clawing his way over the back of the seat to get to help but it was too late. By now Cody had control of the sixty-cal. and worked to clear the jam as he turned it on the other two Jeeps.

The first driver saw but didn't turn in time. Cody raked it with withering fire, shredding the radiator, windshield and tires with a punishing volley. The second Jeep came around, seemingly intent on an attack, before deciding the better of it and careening off. He chased it with a volley of fire until it disappeared behind a ridge.

A cry went up from the assembled Bedouin. Ibn-Melik strode over to clasp Cody's forearm when he clambered down from the Jeep. He spoke seriously and at length in Arabic. Cody didn't understand a word, but he got the old man's tone. The old chieftain recognized what Cody had done for him and his men. And he would not forget.

CHAPTER SEVENTEEN

SOONER OR LATER, Sara thought, hand on the steering wheel as she sat parked in a busy Paris street, *Aisha is bound to wind up here.*

It made perfect sense. Aisha was a young woman under threat. Until approximately two days ago, she had had Cody and Sara to rely on for protection. But she had given that up to go on the run. Where else could she go? Certainly not back to her family. Her brother Achmed's brutal efforts to locate and return her to the Emirates spoke for themselves. There was no going back home. Which left the Order of World Harmony. Sara had been casing the Paris headquarters on and off for the past six hours without luck.

Aisha had originally left home for DC with the express intent of meeting Thelma Justice, Ms. 'World Harmony' herself. Sara knew of the woman's reputation, of course. You couldn't turn on the boob tube without seeing a commercial for her latest book or some cause or product she was sponsoring. Thelma Justice was ubiquitous. She was also a stereotypical female type that Sara herself couldn't stand — the type of woman who projected a motherly, caring persona as a means of getting others to let down their guard.

Like Aunt Kathy. Sara smirked at the memory. As she watched pedestrians streaming by the steel and glass lobby of the OWH headquarters building across the street, she remembered the summer she had been sent to Nebraska to spend a few weeks with Aunt Kathy and Uncle Karl. Karl had been such a poor, browbeaten example of masculinity that, at first, she had been puzzled. But then she had watched Aunt Kathy do her number on everyone around her, deploying her massive mommy angel wings to draw folks in, comfort, enfold and then snare them within her emotional orbit. While seeming sweet as apple pie, Aunt Kathy used people — sucked them dry of emotion, pride and purpose, then wrung them out like old washcloths. Seeing Thelma Justice made Sara ponder that similar tactics could be used to build a business empire.

She checked her watch. It was late and she was hungry. She decided to give it another two hours of surveillance before returning to the youth hostel where she'd registered under a false name and grab a few hours sleep. She opted for some street food and left the car, walking up the block toward the brioche stand near the subway entrance. The stand was a bit of a hike, but she could still keep an eye on the lobby as she went. The doorway was guarded by a uniformed member of Thelma Justice's private female army of security guards called Furies. She was wondering how the OWH managed to obtain permission for their operatives to carry firearms in different countries when she saw Carstairs.

Jesus!

Sara took two quick steps and disappeared behind a bus-stop shelter before he saw her.

It was Carstairs. No doubt about it. The man sitting in the car, eyes fixed on the OWH building while holding the camera with the elephantine telephoto lens was one of CIA's operatives in-country. And Sara knew him.

Carstairs had been working the Paris desk since the late 1980s. Fat, bespectacled, middle-aged and gifted with a marginal intellect at best, he was one of the Agency's "bad bargains" – Cold War agents past their prime yet too young for retirement and too computer illiterate to do much beyond minor surveillance. Carstairs kept getting shuffled from department to department within the Paris station, the espiocrats just biding their time until he could be put out to pasture. Watching the Order of World Harmony seemed a harmless enough assignment.

Unless, he's keeping watch for me.

It seemed the likeliest explanation. Parnell back at CIA had a hate on for her and Cody and was likely onto the OWH's alliance with Vetrov. Watching the place made sense. It was an annoyance. But if there was any mercy in the world, at least the Fates had decreed that poor Carstairs was the genius with whom she'd have to match wits.

She'd seen him before he'd seen her. There was that.

But how to get back to her car?

She kept to the far edge of the sidewalk, close by the shop doorways and made it to the *brioche* cart. She ordered coffee and a croissant, keeping an eye on Carstairs in the reflection of a bath and body shop display window. She was still thinking when a young woman in torn jeans and dreadlocks asked Sara for spare change. An idea occurred to her.

"How would you like to earn ten francs?" she asked.

The girl narrowed her eyes and studied Sara. "Uh, I don't fuck women... Unless, I mean, if you and your husband want a threesome or..."

"Nothing like that." Sara produced a ten franc note from her wallet and tore it in half. "See that fat bald guy in the car over there?"

The girl looked at Carstairs. "Yeah."

"Go over and knock on his window. When he rolls it down, ask him if his name is Carstairs. Tell him you heard the guard in the lobby across the street say she recognized him and called the cops."

The girl raised her eyebrows. "That's it? That's all?"

"C'est tout." Sara smiled.

The girl shrugged, accepted the torn banknote and wandered over to the car. As Sara watched, she knocked, bent when the window rolled down and spoke to Carstairs. She pointed to the lobby where the Fury stood, spoke again and straightened. A moment later, the car started and Carstairs pulled into traffic, narrowly missing a Peugeot, which honked angrily. The girl in dreads watched him peel off down the street before returning to Sara.

"Thanks," she said, handing over the rest of the note.

"That was fun!" The girl laughed. "Is he some kind of peeping tom or something?"

"Something like that." Sara sipped her coffee. "The thing is, you never can tell anymore. The stranger you speak to on the street could end up working for the CIA. You can never be too careful these days."

CHAPTER EIGHTEEN

CODY NOTICED a palpable difference in the air as the camel train approached the Jordanian border. Patrols became less frequent and more scattered. Overflights became rarer – likely the Syrian government's way of avoiding confrontation with the ruthlessly effective and merciless Jordanian Air Force. The land itself seemed to flatten out and become gentler. At one point, a military helicopter with Jordanian markings that was making an overflight of the border region stopped and switched direction when it saw them. Cody grew nervous until he saw how the pilot carefully kept sufficient distance and altitude to avoid spooking the camels. Upon seeing ibn-Melik and his men, the chopper pilot threw a jaunty wave and peeled off, unconcerned.

So the Bedouin are considered friendlies out this way, Cody thought. He had encountered similar experiences with the indigenous peoples of the Arctic. To the Eskimo, there was no difference between a seal hunting ground in northern Canada or northern Russia, and the coast guards of both countries seemed resigned to this fact. The Bedouin, like other wild creatures, were migratory. Cody felt a wave of wistfulness at the notion.

Free people roaming free, he thought. And wondered hos much longer such a lifestyle could withstand the onslaught of 'civilization'.

Shortly before 10 AM by Cody's watch, the camel train topped a rise overlooking a border checkpoint. There wasn't much to the crossing – just a red and yellow swing barrier on the road, a small hut beside it and a border soldier sitting in a chair and reading a comic book, his AK propped against the wall of the hut. He looked up when ibn-Melik and his men approached. Cody watched the headman gracefully guide his mount down the dune into the depression where the checkpoint lay and then up the dune on the opposite side, ignoring the checkpoint and road. This didn't seem to bother the soldier one bit, who smiled and waved cheerfully, eliciting a nod from ibn-Melik. It was obvious that the Bedouin and their migratory ways were well-known to the Jordanian military, who had instructions not to interfere with their peregrinations.

They crossed into Jordanian territory. Cody heard a genuine sigh of relief from young Abdul in the seat ahead of him. The young man turned, grinned at Cody and said something in Arabic that sounded for all the world like "welcome to Jordan." Cody was breathing a little easier, too.

Much as they had in Syria, the camel train kept to the desert, their path occasionally encountering evidence of the modern world. After an hour, they crested a rise and gazed down into the parking lot of a huge, big-box store similar to a Walmart. A toddler watched solemnly from the back seat of his mother's car as ibn-Melik led his troop across an edge of the lot and then over another rise to disappear back into the desert.

There were more highways in Jordan. Cody could hear the hiss of distant traffic as they made their way across the sand, occasionally encountering a ribbon of concrete stretching through the vast terrain. The camels simply trotted along, seemingly unimpressed by the modern vehicles and definitely not frightened of them.

Their path eventually intersected with a highway rest-stop. Ibn-Melik brought the camel train to a halt. That's when Cody noted the lone car parked in the rest-stop lot and the man waiting there.

Clad in a black suit, the man stood by a late model Chevy with his hands clasped behind his back. As they approached, Cody could see he was Oriental. Something in his stance and facial features suggested Japan. He had had prior contact, albeit brief, with Japan's small but highly efficient secret service. With his slicked back hair, dark suit and quiet demeanor, this man reminded him of the agents he had met. When he spoke, the accent confirmed him as Japanese.

"Jack Cody?" The man gave a reticent bow. "I am Hiroto Ishigawa. Hamid Hassan sent me to wait for you. Welcome to Jordan."

"Backchannel?" Cody asked.

"Oss." Ishigawa bowed again.

Cody turned to Abdul. "Thank you," he said quietly. The boy smiled and nodded.

Cody dismounted and presented himself before ibn-Melik. "Thank you, ibn-Melik." Cody offered a shallow bow. "I am forever in your debt. *Salaam.*"

The Bedouin elder smiled down at Cody, nodded and then guided the camel troop off into the sands. Soon, the desert swallowed them.

"I am with Japanese embassy," Ishigawa explained quietly. As they got into the man's Chevy, Cody recognized the man's seniority. Like many Japanese, Ishigawa had aged gracefully but looked to be on the high side of seventy. "Formerly with intelligence service. Good friend of Horace Parsons in Moscow."

"That's great," Cody said, and meant it. The informal group of retired intelligence operatives from Backchannel had been providing him with unfailing support in his mission. Knowing that would continue with Ishigawa was a comfort. Cody wondered what sort of accommodations the man had arranged for him. He hoped a bath and a fridge full of beer might be part of the bargain.

"We go." Ishigawa started the ignition. "You get shower. Food. Then we figure out rest of mission."

"A hot shower and a meal sound great right now, to be honest."

"You travel in desert." Ishigawa gave Cody's rumpled clothes a visual once-over. "Very unsanitary."

"I suppose it is."

"No problem." Ishigawa yanked open the glove compartment and produced a container of sani-wipes. "Please."

"Okay. Thanks." Cody pulled a fresh towelette loose and began wiping his hands. The tissue was soon black with dust.

I must be dirtier than I thought, he realized, pulling another one loose.

Ishigawa, as if sensing that he was being too stiff and formal, attempted to loosen things up. "Music. You like music?"

"Sure," said Cody, shrugging. "What have you got?"

"Only the best." Ishigawa patted the stereo console

lovingly. "I like American music very much. Contemporary classics. Particularly movie soundtracks."

"Modern, huh?"

"Very." The man cracked the barest trace of a smile. "Always up to date."

With that, Ishigawa punched the PLAY button and the mellow sounds of "Raindrops Keep Falling on My Head" filled the car as they plunged down the highway to the capital.

CHAPTER NINETEEN

IN THE COMMERCIAL terminal of Damascus International Airport, a lone janitor passed a vacuum back and forth across the faded reception rug. A man entered the building, wearing an orange jumpsuit emblazoned with the logo of Tellerman International Courier Service. The man in the jumpsuit was obviously a local, something unusual enough to earn him a quizzical look from the janitor. The jumpsuited man responded with a friendly wave before making his way down the concourse toward one of the commercial gateways.

The hard-eyed woman behind the counter was dressed like a stewardess. But something in her stance, in the hardness of her eyes gave her away as something other than what she appeared to be. The man presented himself before her, handed over a small booklet and waited as she examined it. The woman noted the code sequence hidden in amongst the text, confirmed the man was one of theirs and handed back the booklet.

"Through there," she said in Arabic, indicating the doorway behind her.

The man nodded and stepped past her. Passing through the doorway, he entered a long, windowless hallway that ended at an open door. Another woman, similarly dressed, stood waiting there. The man in the orange jumpsuit presented the booklet a second time and this woman scanned it for the code, just like the first. Satisfied, she closed the book, handed it back and told the man to follow the walkway outside. Beyond the door was a path resembling a crosswalk that someone had marked on the tarmac in yellow paint.

The man in the jumpsuit followed the yellow path, which was guarded by a security guard holding a machine-gun. The guard watched the man carefully as he traversed the path, following it to a small commercial freight jet parked outside the terminal. The man in orange reached the bottom of the steps and climbed. A woman attired similarly to the two inside was waiting at the top.

"*Salaam aleikum,*" said the man. He pointed to himself. "Ibrahim Fata."

The woman checked his name on a list and then handed him a black plastic lunchbox. "Don't open it until you are told to," she cautioned him in Arabic. The man nodded and took a seat on the bench she pointed to.

Five minutes passed. Then another man, also wearing an orange jumpsuit with the Tellerman Courier logo boarded the plane. The woman went through the same routine with him, checking his name, handing him the lunchbox and warning, then sending him to sit on the bench.

Over the course of the next half-hour, five more men entered the plane, gave their names, received their lunchbox and took a seat. After the seventh man had been seated, the "flight attendant" closed the hatch and disappeared up front to the cockpit. Soon after, the jet's engines rumbled to life and the aircraft began taxiing for take-off. As one, the men strapped into their bench harnesses and waited.

After an interminable wait, the engines' tone shifted upward and became a shriek. Then they were plunging down the runway, the sights outside obscured by the windowless bulkheads. The men on the benches knew the plane had taken off when the rumble beneath the wheels fell away and the downward pressure of lift-off pressed them into their seats.

A short time later, the woman reappeared, now dressed in a sort of military uniform. She went to a control panel on the bulkhead, lifted a phone from its bracket and began speaking in Arabic.

"Our first stop is Athens," she said. "We will be in the air for approximately two hours. The first of you will debark there and follow the same procedures each of the rest of you will follow in your respective destinations. Please open your packages."

The men fell to fumbling with the catches and lids of their black plastic lunchboxes. The contents of each were identical: a cellphone, a numbered key and a Styrofoam cube about the size of a baseball.

"Upon arrival, you will go to the airport lockers. The number on the key identifies your locker. You will open the locker, remove the suitcase inside and go to the men's room where you will change into the regular clothing provided for you. Inside each suitcase is also an envelope containing cash, the name of a hotel and a room key. You will take a taxi to the hotel, walk right past the registration desk and up to your room. You each have a reservation for a two week stay.

"You will enter the room, lock the door and remain there. Arrangements have been made to provide room service meals twice daily. You will not leave the room under any circumstances until you are instructed to do so.

"The phone is set to receive calls only. You cannot call from the phone. Keep the phone by your side at all times. Answer immediately when it rings. Go wherever the voice at the other end tells you to go. Bring the Styrofoam cube with you. You will be told what to do with it at that time.

"Now please close your packages and remain silent for the remainder of the flight."

The woman hung up.

The men said nothing as the jet winged its way northwest. Soon they were out over the Mediterranean. The flight progressed smoothly, without turbulence, and crossed the ocean without incident. Then it began its descent.

The plane landed in Athens. The woman returned to the phone and addressed the group.

"Ibrahim Fata."

The first man to have boarded the plane rose, lunchbox in hand and exited through the hatch. He descended the steps and disappeared into the terminal building. Then the hatch was buttoned up and the plane taxied into place for departure.

Two hours later, it landed in Rome and another man deplaned. Then it was off to its next stop.

CHAPTER TWENTY

SARA TOOK to haunting the neighborhood where the Order of World Harmony was headquartered.

It made sense to continue surveillance on the building. It was the one lead she had. The tracer continued to identify the office block as the nexus around which Aisha's red dot kept hovering. Rather than take off and pursue the girl directly, risking exposure and the chance of spooking her, Sara purchased a few differently colored hoodies and hats and rotated through them, repositioning herself at various places from which she could watch the building throughout the day.

In the mornings, she haunted the nearby news kiosk and subway entrance. As the morning commuter crowds thinned out, she would relocate to a nearby café and nurse a brioche and coffee as she continued her vigil. By the time that was finished, the early lunch crowd would be streaming in. Sara took advantage of the flow to return to her car, change and relocate.

Two doors down from the café was a bookstore. Not one of those charming, dilapidated French book stalls with the weathered façade but a multi-floor chain outlet. The stacks at the second floor ended at a window where Sara could stand unobtrusively with her nose in a book, one eye on the street below. As such, she didn't notice the dark-haired woman hovering nearby for nearly twenty minutes. But the moment she did, her senses were on alert.

Sara studied the woman surreptitiously. Dark hair, full lips, clad in an expensive pantsuit and heels, she looked like an executive or business owner. It was obvious, from the way she moved, that she was not a trained operative – that would have been obvious within a minute or two. But there was no doubt she had her eye on Sara.

Maybe she's just some lonely Paris lesbian, Sara thought. With a sigh, she replaced the copy of the Houllebecq novel she had been pretending to study on its shelf and rounded the end of the aisle, putting a row of shelves between herself and the dark-haired woman as she made for the stairs. She moved quickly, head down, trying to appear like a worker eager to return to her desk after lunch hour. She had her hand on the banister and was about to take a step when a voice spoke behind her.

"Excuse me…"

English? Sara pretended not to hear. She took another step, then a hand touched her shoulder.

"Excuse me. I'm sorry, but… Can I speak to you for a minute?"

The light touch, the apology, the public approach… All these things combined to modify Sara's trained instinct to grab and break the hand, then flee. She turned to find the woman standing on the step beside her.

"I know you don't know me," she said in English.

"My name is Tiff Butler. I'm a journalist. And I couldn't help noticing…"

"My ass? Listen, lady. I'm not into girls." She made a dismissive gesture. "Why don't you try one of the bars down by the river?"

At this, the woman laughed. "No, I'm… I mean I'm not trying to pick you up or make a pass at you. I just…" She cut her eyes toward the window at the end of the aisle. "I've noticed you hanging around here for the past day or so. Because I'm doing the same thing."

"You have no idea what I'm doing."

"Watching the door of the building across the street." Tiff Butler said this with a slow cat-smile. "The European headquarters of the Order of World Harmony. I'm doing research for an exposé I'm writing about the group."

"Well, good luck with it." Sara turned and continued descending the stairs.

"My area of interest has to do with celebrities who have been drawn into the Order." Tiff Butler was following her now. "You know, Thelma Justice is popular among movie stars and other prominently placed people…"

Sara grunted.

"Including the Princess Aisha from the Emirates."

Sara reached the bottom of the stairs and kept moving, pretending the name meant nothing to her. But inside, her guts were churning. *Aisha?* How did this woman know…?

"I don't know if you're aware of this, but…" Tiff Butler flicked her eyes back and forth, ensuring others were out of earshot, "Princess Aisha is an ardent devotee of Thelma Justice and her movement. So much so that she *ran away* from her family home to attend a rally in DC."

A sickening feeling in Sara's stomach caused her guts to plunge.

"She was at the center of a violent attack that occurred there."

"I read about that," Sara said. She had slowed, now allowed herself to pause.

"I was the one who broke the story." Tiff Butler was studying her now, weighing the impact of each word as she spoke it. "Princess Aisha disappeared soon after the incident. A great deal was hushed up afterwards… All my law enforcement and private security contacts suddenly dried up after the story was published. There's something more than meets the eye going on. I have reason to believe Princess Aisha may be there now. That she may have taken refuge and been given sanctuary by Thelma Justice's movement."

"So you're watching the place."

"And noticed you doing the same." Tiff Butler gave a slightly defeated shrug. "It was worth a chance, talking to you. I'm sorry if I intruded…" She turned to go.

Sara, her mind churning, sorted through a half-dozen possible responses before…

"Wait."

Tiff Butler turned.

"Uh, I'm sorry." Sara smiled. "I appreciate the info. Maybe we should talk some more."

"Sure." The woman's face took on an expression of concern. "There's a pretty decent café around the corner. Let me buy you lunch, and we can compare notes."

Sara considered the woman and her offer carefully. She had no reason to believe Tiff Butler was anything other than what she claimed to be. She saw no indications of backup or bodyguards anywhere nearby. And she knew that, if necessary, she could effect a swift escape. So far as she could tell, Tiff Butler presented no immediate danger.

And she may have information about Aisha…

Deciding she had nothing to lose, Sara shrugged. "Sure." She smiled. "Why not?"

CHAPTER TWENTY-ONE

ISHIGAWA AND CODY took the highway into Jordan's capital, Amman. But rather than turn toward the glittering clutch of high-rise towers that housed the business district, the Japanese steered into a tired and run-down section of town. Not exactly a bad neighborhood, but one that obviously changed character after dark. Along one side of the street, a row of shops was closing for the day, the merchants drawing displays of fruit, stacks of linen, racks of newspapers in off the sidewalk and rolling down the metal shutters that protected their shop windows. A few seemed to recognize Ishigawa as he parked at the curb and got out. The sign on the door of the modest establishment there was lettered in both Western and Arabic script.

ISHIGAWA IMPORTS & EXPORTS

Ishigawa exchanged pleasantries with the shopkeeper next door before conducting Cody inside. The vestibule was a cramped space maybe twice the size of a washroom on a commercial airliner. Cody noted how Ishigawa carefully locked and double-bolted the door behind them. For all Ishigawa's cordiality, Cody doubted any of his fellow shopkeepers had been invited inside for a visit.

"Please." Ishigawa smiled, opened a narrow doorway in the opposite wall and motioned Cody through.

Cody entered a low-ceilinged, narrow hallway that extended straight back what must have been the rear wall of the building. There was a ladder placed there. At Ishigawa's urging, Cody climbed up into a small furnished office. A narrow rear window let out onto the alley behind the store. That was when Cody realized what Ishigawa had done with the place.

He's stripped out the interior and doubled the space inside, he realized. The distance between ceiling and floor had been reduced such that Cody guessed the two-story structure now had three or more floors. With the wooden beams and polished wood floors, the place had the feel of an old wooden sailing ship from the 19th century. It was a rabbit warren, but an exceptionally tidy, well-built one.

Ishigawa took a seat at a narrow desk. On a table to one side was a hot plate with a tea kettle on the ring. As Ishigawa prepared tea, he invited Cody to take a seat in the guest chair. Once they were settled with China cups of green tea, Ishigawa drew a folder across the desk towards him and opened it.

"According to our friend Hamid, the terrorist group Crimson Jihad suffered a massacre." He studied the page. "Almost one thousand were killed in a mass helicopter strike."

"I was there. Thanks to Hamid, I narrowly escaped with my life. If Crimson Jihad is losing numbers, I can't see that as anything but a positive development."

"Ah. Apparently, White Wolf ordered the strike himself." Ishiagawa's mouth firmed as he took up a photograph and passed it across the desk. "Evidence found of Russian munitions being used."

"Vetrov." Cody's fist clenched of its own volition. He studied the photograph. A scattering of charred and broken bodies littered the floor of the valley. "They were Russian choppers. And Vetrov was there. Question is – if they're working together, then why...?"

"I may have answer." Ishigawa searched through the folder again. "Syrian intelligence issued an alert for two men. Both Crimson Jihad, both spotted at Damascus Airport two days after the massacre. Here..." He extended a fax copy of a Syrian police bulletin. Cody couldn't read the Arabic script but noted the photos showing two men in orange jumpsuits captured by CCTV.

"What's this?" Cody pointed to the patch on the jumpsuits.

"Tellerman International Courier Service. I checked." Ishigawa smiled apologetically. "Company does not exist."

"So it's a front." Cody's eyes narrowed. "The White Wolf kills off the majority of his force in-country and then exfiltrates a small number of men abroad. The killings probably to maintain operational secrecy and serve as a distraction." Cody reflected that a man would have to be a major psychopath to kill off his own for such a reason. "Whatever he's planning, it must be big."

"Tellerman flight from Damascus flew to Athens. Then Rome. Here is the flight plan."

Cody examined the third page Ishigawa handed him. The flight had played quite the game of hopscotch across the EU, making seven stops in major capitals.

"You've got encrypted Wi-Fi here?" Cody produced his cellphone.

"*Hai*. Yes."

Cody fired off a text message to Sara in France. One of the White Wolf's men had apparently made it to Paris. She would want to know.

"I have to get into Europe," he told Ishigawa. "My partner is there tracking down the Princess Aisha. And now the White Wolf's men are there. I can kill two birds with one stone if I start in Italy. I'll see if I can track down the White Wolf's man in Rome and see what's being planned. I also know Thelma Justice has a presence in that country. Can you help me?"

Ishigawa smiled. "I can." He rose and gestured toward a low door. "Please, Cody-san."

Cody slid aside the wooden panel door and stepped through into another small, cabin-like room. This one was decorated in a more traditional Japanese fashion. Backlit shoji screens bathed the room in a gentle low light. Cody spotted shelves with *bonsai* trees along one wall. A low lacquer table sat in the middle of the room surrounded by an inert forest of metal machinery.

As Cody watched, Ishigawa disappeared behind a panel screen and emerged a minute later, his jacket and tie replaced by a thick printer's apron. He gestured for Cody to take a seat in a chair across the table from him. As Cody did, the Japanese opened a drawer in a nearby cabinet and began placing items on the table: an ink pad, stamps and some sort of sewing kit. He spoke quietly as he did this.

"We will arrange for you to enter Italy via Genoa," he said. He was opening a package of heavy linen paper with a razor-sharp dagger. "Backchannel's resources in Italy suffered a terrible setback. We have no one on the ground there. So I make you a proper Italian passport. That way there are no questions."

And to Cody's amazement, Ishigawa began carefully and painstakingly creating a perfect simulacrum of an Italian EU passport. Fingers moving with origami grace, he folded and set pages, aligned watermarks, created a booklet by hand. This was the true forger's art – creation of false official documents with everyday materials, a craft all but lost in the age of internet and ink-jet printers. As in sword-fighting, calligraphy or sushi-making, the Japanese had made of forgery an art form from a relatively commonplace activity. Ishigawa measured, cut and combined a set of thick pages which he began sewing together with book binder's thread.

"What setback did Backchannel suffer?" Cody had benefitted from Backchannel's informal network of retired agents, who had been instrumental in helping him and Sara in their pursuit of Vetrov and Thelma Justice. His contact Jacquard back in Monte Carlo had been killed in the line of duty.

"Our man in Rome was killed by members of a rival service." Ishigawa was trimming and tightening the book binder's thread as he spoke. "It appears to have been the work of a group operating out of the Vatican."

The same group that killed Jacquard. "So they're conducting a purge."

"So it seems."

Cody bore this firmly in mind. When he landed in Genoa he would be alone. And absolutely in enemy territory.

CHAPTER TWENTY-TWO

"It has begun." The White Wolf slapped a hand down on the polished conference table. "My men will soon be in place in fifty capital cities across the globe. Everything has gone according to plan."

Thelma Justice and Greb Vetrov traded a look. Outside the tall glass windows of the conference room, the Syrian sands stretched into the distance. But here in the office building once owned by a French oil company, all was cool and shaded in half-light. Their plan was coming along right on schedule. It was coming time to move on to Phase 2.

"Everything has been put in place for your men by my organization," said Thelma. "They will be sheltered and fed until the time comes for them to deliver their packages."

"Those also have been provided." Vetrov flicked a glance her way. "Sealed vials inside Styrofoam containers taped shut. When the time comes, they remove the tape, open the vials and deploy the sample inside."

"And the man delivering the sample?" Thelma asked. "What happens to him?"

"Instant contamination," said Vetrov.

"With their part of the plan executed, they will no longer be needed." The White Wolf waved a hand. "They go to paradise as martyrs. *Inshallah.*"

"That neatly ties up any loose ends," she admitted.

"I will be ready to give the signal at your word." The White Wolf produced a cellphone and held it aloft. "I have all fifty of the numbers programmed here. We can activate individual operatives or send them all at once."

"We'll see," said Thelma. "Depending on how the rest of the plan goes."

"Yes." The White Wolf pocketed the phone and leaned across the table toward them, balancing on his fists. "The rest of the plan. The hammer from on high."

"It's time to tell him," said Vetrov.

Thelma Justice nodded. "I agree."

"You said somebody highly placed in their defense apparatus would help you turn their weapons against them. This is the plan?"

"It is." Thelma Justice pulled her briefcase onto her lap and opened it. "This is not generally known. In fact, less than a dozen people at the highest levels of the US defense infrastructure are aware of the existence of this project. The entire thing has been carried out in strictest compartmentalization over the course of three presidents' terms. But last month, RaptorNet went live."

She fished a document from her briefcase and placed it on the table. It was an artist's rendering of a ring of identical satellites orbiting the Earth.

"RaptorNet began life as a launch redundancy system. At least, that's how it was explained to me," said Thelma. "In the event of a nuclear war, the ability to launch countermeasures if you are attacked first is key. RaptorNet was originally designed to provide that advantage. That's when it occurred to the defense analysts that the system could functionally *replace* the US launch infrastructure."

"Now all US missiles are launched by signal from satellites," said Vetrov, tapping the photo.

"Unlike the old system, this one relies strictly on digital protocols. That triggering system was designed by Dr. Clarence Nodwell of MIT." Thelma smiled. "Dr. Nodwell is very much ours to do with as we please."

"The hammer from on high." The White Wolf nodded. "I understand. So you will use this man, this Dr. Nodwell, to gain access to those weapons and turn them against the Infidels, against America. Our common enemy."

Vetrov nodded. "Exactly."

"To what end?" The White Wolf narrowed his eyes. "For the warriors of Islam, the goal is logical and obvious. But less so with you." He nodded to Thelma. "You are not Muslim. And neither is General Vetrov. What is your goal in all of this?"

Vetrov and Thelma Justice exchanged a look.

"Isn't destroying our common enemy goal enough for you?" she said aloud. But inside she was thinking:

Better keep an eye on this one. He could be dangerous to us.

CHAPTER TWENTY-THREE

AT TIFF BUTLER'S URGING, she and Sara killed the remainder of that evening and early night hiding out in a cineplex. The place had eight screens, so the two women were able to sit through two showings of the latest *Star Wars* saga before ducking into the washroom and then into some Italian comedy, which ran until nearly midnight. Then they went in search of a woman Tiff said had contacts inside the Order of World Harmony.

It took an hour of walking thorough the narrow backstreets of Paris. Sara could tell by the changing altitude and rooftop architecture that they were approaching the Seine. Once Tiff judged the moment right and the coast clear, they emerged onto a broad avenue of cafes and tiny shopfronts. Sara recognized the Le Marais neighborhood, well known for its gay and lesbian club scene. Tiff led them across the street to the tall, pavilion-style entrance to one called Le petit chat. Sara stopped at the curb.

"Wait. In there?"

"What's the matter?" Tiff bared her teeth in a teasing smile. "Scared a lesbian might bite you?"

Sara laughed. "Alright," she said, still chuckling. "Sure, let's go in."

Sara had never been one for the club scene. And the company of gay and lesbian people left her as cold as that of conservative straight people with two-point-five kids and a white picket fence. In truth, there were very few social haunts Sara felt comfortable inhabiting. The gym, maybe. Happy hour among fellow spooks and military people. *But a lesbian dance club?* Deciding it made sense someone connected to an all-female organization might hang out there, she followed Tiff Butler inside.

The entrance led into a hallway fashioned after an amusement park "tunnel of love" ride. A bouncer at the end, a massive black woman in a muscle T-shirt, sat on a stool checking IDs. She looked up as they approached.

"Five Euro cover charge," she said. "Unless you're here to fight."

"Fight?" Surprised, the word was out of Sara's mouth before she realized she'd spoken.

"Yep. Oil wrestling night," replied the bouncer. "Bring a bikini and I waive the surcharge."

"That's fine," said Tiff, leaning in with a ten Euro bill. "We're here to see Colette."

"Colette." The bouncer accepted the tenner and put it in a cigar box at the podium, then leaned forward to stamp their hands. "She'll be down at the pit. You'll find her in Tati's corner."

"Thanks." Tiff waited until Sara's hand had been stamped before seizing it and pulling her into the club. "Cover," she whispered, squeezing Sara's hand. "This way no one will hit on us."

"I have to pretend to be your girlfriend. Great!"

Sara sighed. She was no more attracted to women than she was to drywall or stones piled by the roadside. Lesbians frankly mystified her, but Tiff's plan made sense. So she returned the hand pressure, squared her shoulders and tried to think of famous lesbians she could imitate just to look the part. She was having a mental block.

Inside the place was loud, poorly lit and stank of cigarette smoke. A few dozen rowdy lesbians were cheering on two bikini-clad women oil wrestling in an inflatable wading pool at the center of the room, where a battle royal was under way. A slender blonde with a ponytail and a mean smirk was entwined with a butch Oriental girl whose black hair was styled in a pageboy cut. Both were flexing, struggling and trying like hell to strangle or arm-twist each other into submission. Cheers flared amid grunts of effort as oil splashed high.

Sara saw a few of the women turn to check her out as she passed. *Billie Jean King,* she told herself. *Just be Billie Jean King.*

There was one woman, however, that wouldn't stop staring. Sara gritted her teeth and did her best to ignore her. The woman was bald and black, slender and dressed in a pair of overalls. She caught sight of Sara and apparently fell in love because her eyes bugged wide, and she began following her through the crowd. Sara leaned in and mentioned this to Tiff.

"Don't worry," she laughed. "I'll protect you!"

They were at the corner of the wading pool now and the oil wrestlers were taking a break. Tiff Butler stole up behind a woman who was rubbing the shoulders of the tired and achey Oriental contender. She spoke briefly before the woman, presumably Colette, turned and nodded toward a door in back.

Tiff returned, grabbed Sara's hand and made for the door.

"She'll meet us in here," Tiff whispered. As Sara paused behind her, waiting for Tiff to turn the handle, she scanned the crowd. *No sign of Overalls,* she thought, and that was good.

The doorway led into a large storeroom. Dimly lit, it contained shelves that extended into the spaces toward the ceiling crammed with canned goods, cans and bottles of alcohol, cutlery, table sundries. The place also did double duty as a utility closet. Sara noted a janitor's station, with mops and cleaning solutions. *That'll be used to clean up after tonight's oil-o-rama,* she thought.

A minute or two passed before Colette, a large-boned brunette woman, let herself in by the same door. She greeted Tiff with a hug and favored Sara with a nod.

"This is Sara," Tiff said. "She's the woman I told you about."

"Right." Colette's English was heavily accented. "So you said. The curious one."

"The one asking all the questions."

The voice came from behind them. Sara turned and saw Overalls stalking up behind her, followed by the two wrestlers from the oil pit. All were glaring at her.

"What—?" Sara turned back to see Tiff pointing a small automatic at her.

"Get her!" snarled Colette.

Overalls sprang, grasping for Sara. But Sara dropped her center of gravity, met Overalls' wrists in mid-grab and deflected her. She managed to pull Overalls off-balance and deliver a sharp elbow-strike to her side. Then the oil wrestlers pounced. Sara had miscalculated the advantage the oil gave them. The girls moved fast, struck hard and each grabbed an arm, wrenching and yanking Sara off-balance.

"Put her on the GROUND!" snapped Colette.

The two wrestlers worked together to flatten Sara chest-first on the concrete storeroom floor. She felt a knee slide across the back of her neck, pinning her in place. Then Overalls was clipping handcuffs into place and chuckling in Sara's ear.

"Thelma Justice can't wait to meet you," she snarled.

CHAPTER TWENTY-FOUR

CODY'S PATH to Genoa was swift but circuitous. Ishigawa adjusted his plan upon learning of the Vatican's involvement in Cody's adventures so far.

"Vatican action service team represents unanticipated risk," he said, referring to the group that had interfered with Cody's efforts in the south of France and was, even now, purging their country of Backchannel operatives. "We will send you in through the back door."

This "back door" involved a flight from Jordan to Cyprus aboard an ancient DC-3 that seemed one loose screw away from falling out of the sky at any moment. Cody had taken a seat in the rear, an anonymous face among the mixed crowd of bureaucrats, holidaymakers and ordinary folk heading for the partitioned island. Someone had even brought a goat onboard. It spent the flight in a crate behind the galley, morosely gobbling hay and snoozing. In Nicosia, he transferred to another ancient plane, this one a de Havilland, which brought him to Corsica. From there, Ishigawa had arranged passage onboard a fishing boat.

Cody spent the duration of his passage in his cabin, poring over the data Ishigawa had given him about the Vatican's action against Backchannel and reflecting on his experiences in France. The Vatican team, whoever they were, had proven every bit as capable as a US special operations force. They had killed the Backchannel operative in Monte Carlo, Jacquard, who had been Cody's and Sara's contact and come perilously close to killing Cody and Sara, too. So far as he could make out, their goal was to intercept the tablet Aisha carried.

The damn tablet, Cody thought. A clay document dating from the First Century AD, it described an alternate Gospel where Jesus had a twin sister named Judith with whom he performed miracles. Not the sort of thing the Vatican would want getting out. But absolutely the sort of thing Thelma Justice, with her female supremacist philosophy, would love to acquire. The tablet somehow played into her plans with Vetrov. Cody's job was to stop them both cold.

He came out on deck as they slid into the harbor at Genoa. The crew of the fishing boat, a forty-foot ketch, bid Cody goodbye as he ambled on deck, looking every inch the Genoan fisherman with his duffel bag, cloth cap and rope-soled sandals. He kept his head down, scanning from the corner of his eye to see whose attention he caught. As it happened, no one aside from a harbor cop who gave him a once over as he strolled out through the main gates to the street beyond. And with that, he was in Italy.

————

No CIA. No Backchannel contact. Not even Sara, who had gone silent on text. Cody reflected on times in the past when he had found himself operational without the usual safety nets. He was accustomed to improvising in hostile territory, but he wasn't about to let the one card he had up his sleeve go unused.

After sending Sara another text, he made the call to Ishigawa in Jordan. The Japanese spook answered on the first ring.

"Cody-san." The smile was evident in the voice. "Hopefully you call from Europe?"

"Italy." Cody glanced out the restroom window of the train. "I should be arriving in Rome here shortly."

"Ah." Ishigawa sorted through papers on his end of the line. "When in Rome, as they say. Do as Romans, yes?" He uttered a gentle laugh. "Cody-san, a friend was able to offer some assistance. A Japanese, like me. Very gifted in computer search."

"A hacker."

"Just so. I offer him a sort of puzzle. What can we learn from the pattern of flights of Tellerman Courier planes? My friend offer very interesting insight."

"What's that?"

"If men are being placed as part of coordinated operation, then operation will not happen immediately. Is impossible, yes? Man arrive in Athens at 9 AM, another in London at 11:30 PM, how can they act as one? No. There must be time delay."

"Makes sense." Cody's pulse began to quicken.

"So. Make sense that hotel reservations be in place. *Special* reservations. Possibly for extended stay. With special considerations. For Muslims? For non-English speakers? For men unfamiliar with technology? I do not know." Again, the gentle laugh. "But I suggest my friend look at hotel reservations. First, he use travel agent software. He isolate hotels with extended booking capability.

Then he take a chance and – how you say? *Hack* into computer system of three hotels."

"What did he find?" Cody grinned. Ishigawa was one smart guy.

"We have one man registered at Hilton Hotel in Rome. Two weeks stay. Special instructions to provide meals twice per day every day for two weeks." Ishigawa cleared his throat. "This seems to be a good candidate for you to investigate."

Ishigawa, I love you! thought Cody. "What's the room number?"

"436."

Cody memorized the number. "Thank you, Ishigawa-san. That is unbelievably helpful."

"You are welcome. What will you do?"

"I think I'll stop in and pay the guy a visit."

"Very good idea. Be sure to bring gift." Cody thought he heard Ishigawa smile. "Is ancient Japanese tradition."

CHAPTER TWENTY-FIVE

SARA CAME to in groggy waves of consciousness. At some point in the proceedings, they had pressed a rag doused with chloroform to her mouth. The last thing she remembered was being dragged outside by Colette and Overalls and loaded into a van. Then she passed out.

Remembering her SERE training, she was careful to keep eyes closed and her breathing calm. Her ability to survive, evade, resist and escape would depend on her ability to control her reactions to her captors. She concentrated on her immediate surroundings. Sound? There was a noise like an air conditioner. Feel? She lay on something soft, a texture of silk beneath her fingers. Smell? She recognized the odor of Aisha's patchouli and opened her eyes.

She was lying on her back in what appeared for all the world to be some sort of hotel room. The bed beneath her, the rubberized curtains drawn against the light, the TV and suitcase stand, and adjoining bathroom all suggested accommodations. Only the absence of a doorknob on the entryway door gave a hint to their actual predicament. And then there was Aisha.

She sat on the edge of the bed, hands folded, watching Sara with a kind of calm expectancy.

"Where are we?" Sara blinked, clearing the cobwebs and fought to sit up.

"We are in Italy." Aisha spoke quietly, her eyes diverted. Her posture bore the heraldry of discomfort and shame. "This facility is in the northern part of the country. In the mountains."

"And it belongs to Thelma Justice."

"Of course."

Sara felt a stab of anger. "What the hell did you *do*, Aisha?"

The girl drew a breath to answer and then disintegrated. She bowed her head and began weeping, shoulders shaking, releasing great gusting sobs with each breath. Ordinarily, Sara might have sat up and comforted the girl, at least put an arm around her. But she recalled how the girl had suddenly up and disappeared, abandoning she and Cody in Monte Carlo. The sting of that betrayal had still not yet healed. So Sara remained motionless, waiting for Aisha to get herself under control.

"I …I needed *answers.*" She blinked back tears and wiped her nose on the back of her wrist. "I'm sorry. I – Sara, it's difficult…*impossible* for you to understand the burden the tablet has placed on me! Such an important artifact. *Everyone* wants it!"

"Of course. It's a historical treasure."

"But for *their own reasons!*" Aisha looked up, her expression suddenly fierce. "The Muslim community wants it so they can use it to disprove the Christian

Gospels! The Catholics want it so it can remain hidden! The Americans want it because owning it brings power and influence! The Russians want it for the same reason! Everyone wants it except for the reason it really matters!"

"Which is?"

"The truth!" The words exploded from Aisha's mouth, booming in the room. "Doesn't anybody care about the truth anymore? Doesn't anybody want to know *what really happened?* With Jesus? With His great miracles? You know, we Muslims revere Jesus as a great prophet! *I* revered Him! And I deplore what's been done in His name! And in the name of Islam! And in the name of democracy! And science! All that killing... *That's not God's plan for us!"*

"So you went running to Thelma Justice?" Sara regretted the edge of violent skepticism in her voice. But it was how she felt. "Aisha, the woman is a lunatic! You know she's in deep with General Vetrov! Didn't it occur to you that perhaps she would use you for reasons of her own?"

Aisha said nothing. Merely stared at the carpet and shook her head miserably.

Sara gritted her teeth. She was furious with the girl. But the longer she sat there the more that fury became undercut by a kind of fellow feeling. Understanding began to take hold of Sara. Aisha wasn't a bad kid. She was just...

A kid. Sara studied the girl. She was no more than twenty or so. Where had Sara been at that age? Struggling through life, her first years in the military, trying to figure out money, boys, her personal beliefs and her life goals. Her biggest problem back then had been passing inspection at the academy.

I didn't have an ancient Biblical artifact and an international nuclear arms conspiracy to deal with, she thought. Sara honestly wasn't sure she would have fared any better in Aisha's place.

"Aisha," she said. "Please listen to me."

The girl drew a shuddery breath and gave Sara her full attention.

"There will always be people who claim to have the answer to life's riddles," Sara said. "And life is full of them. Sometimes the answer to one riddle seems to invalidate the answer to another. How do we turn the other cheek to someone trying to kill us? How do we remain charitable in a world where greed is the rule? How do we act with love when there is so much hate? Politics and religion all have their preferred answers. But here's the thing.

"A lot of those answers depend on idealized visions of the future. A Communist worker's paradise or religious one. A world where everyone is morally enlightened. Or what-have-you. But none of those 'answers' acknowledges the simple truth that we live in a competitive, cutthroat world. It's human nature to compete, often unfairly. So in the end we have to pick a side. And if you did anything wrong, Aisha, *that's* what you did. You failed to pick a side. And you've suffered the consequences. We all have."

Aisha, eyes brimming with pain, accepted this with a nod. "I understand," she whispered. "I should have understood the sacrifices you've made on my behalf and the value of my alliance with you and Jack Cody and I did not. I'm sorry."

Sara smiled. In the final analysis, Aisha's was the perfect answer.

"People can grow and change, Aisha," she said quietly. "Take the lesson."

As she spoke, the door rattled. When it opened, Overalls stood there, backed up by two armed Furies.

"Rise and shine," she snickered. "The boss lady wants to see you."

CHAPTER TWENTY-SIX

WEARING a cheap set of coveralls and carrying a toolbox, Cody exited the elevator and began walking down the fourth-floor hallway of the Rome Hilton. The freshly vacuumed hallway was sterile and quiet, the guests ensconced in their rooms behind thick oak doors leaving him free to explore. He walked past room 436, the one inhabited by Hilton's guest here for a two week stay and a rider on his reservation for twice-daily delivery of room service meals.

It was now ten to eight. *Ishigawa said the instructions specify meals at 8 AM and 5 PM,* he thought. Cody found an air duct up the hall from the room, set down the toolbox and bent to unscrew the duct. As he worked, a hotel waiter appeared and pushed a wheeled cart past him toward the room.

"This guy!" snorted the waiter to Cody in Italian, hooking a thumb at the door to 436. "He eats like a horse! Never a scrap on the plate when he's done. Some days, I think I may return to discover he's eaten the napkins!"

Cody chuckled at this unbelievable turn of good luck and played along. "He always eats in the room?"

"Very private!" The waiter halted the cart and lifted a tray of breakfast things, which he set beside the door. "I leave the tray. After I leave, he takes and eats and puts it back in the hallway. Never a scrap left!" Shaking his head, the waiter knocked twice on the door, turned and trundled off down the hallway pushing his cart.

Cody turned his back to the door, positioning the small shaving mirror he'd purchased along with the coveralls on top of his toolbox. Though obscured from behind, it offered him a clear line of site on the door to 436. *Let's get a look at this guy,* he thought.

A long minute elapsed during which he removed one and then started on a second screw. In the distance, the elevator dinged and the waiter with the cart disappeared inside. It was only when the doors rolled closed that the man in 436 made his appearance. In the mirror, Cody saw the door open and the slender face of the dark-skinned man emerge to scan the hallway. The moment he caught sight of Cody, he closed the door, leaving his breakfast in the hall.

That tells me something right there, Cody thought. He dickered with the vent cover for a few more minutes before packing up, pausing to yawn and stretch, ensuring he would be visible to Mr. 436 through his door's peephole before strolling off.

———

He spent the afternoon checking details for the next leg of his trip. He noted the location of Thelma Justice's chateau in the Italian Alps. The place was just up the road from a small, exclusive ski resort that was several hours away by car from the nearest town. There was a company in the region that offered custom helicopter tours. Cody made a note of the name and number and then tried texting Sara again. After two hours, he failed to receive a response.

He was torn. Knowing she was in Paris and unresponsive, he fought the urge to fly there immediately and search for her. *First things first,* he thought. Deal with Vetrov and Thelma. That done, chances were that he'd locate Sara in the process.

But before he could do that, he had Mr. 436 to deal with.

At 4 PM, he entered the lobby of the Hilton bearing a suitcase. His face partially hidden beneath the brim of a broad, wide-brimmed hat, he took the elevator to the fourth floor and wandered down to room 434, directly across the hall from his man.

Certain he was being observed as he did so, he parked his suitcase in front of the door and began fumbling in his pockets. This pantomime effectively concealed his producing his cellphone. A cable snaked from its data port to a credit card-sized rectangle of plastic with a magnetic strip on the back. Cody inserted the card into the keypad door lock and called up an app labeled EN[Y]GMA_7, an NSA cyber-tool identified he had used before to unlock biometric codes and keypad locks. In moments, the door opened, and he let himself inside.

He had rolled the dice and lucked out. The room was unoccupied. Pocketing the phone, he checked his watch. It was 4:07 PM. He pressed his eye to the peephole in the room and watched the door across the hall. For forty minutes, nothing happened. Then a waiter appeared, pushing a cart loaded with a dinner tray.

Right on time, thought Cody.

The waiter put the tray on the floor outside of 436, knocked and departed. Cody counted to thirty before hearing the elevator chime and the sound of trundling as the waiter pushed the cart aboard. Another ten seconds elapsed before 436 opened and the man stepped into the hall and bent for the tray.

Cody ripped open the door, lunged across the hall and tackled the man, spilling the contents of the dinner tray across the hallway carpet. The man opened his mouth to scream but two quick punches knocked loose some teeth as well as any impulse to make further noise. Cody dragged him into 436 and shut the door. Then he drew his Beretta and leveled it on the man.

"Don't move." He flicked off the safety. "I can put a bullet in you and be gone before anyone knows I was ever here. What's your name?"

The man, hands raised, was bug-eyed with fear. Cody saw a terrified impulse to comply with whatever was being requested of him. But it was obvious he had no idea what Cody was saying. A few more language stabs in French and Arabic fared no better, leading Cody to surmise this one was likely from one of the more remote villages in the Middle East – the type ripe for recruiting by the White Wolf.

"White Wolf," he said in Arabic and the man's eyes jumped in recognition.

Good enough.

He gestured with the pistol, telling the man to roll over and lay on his stomach. When he did, Cody secured his wrists using a towel from the bathroom. After stuffing a washcloth in the guy's mouth, he set about searching the room.

The man had obviously brought nothing with him

but the clothes in his suitcase. A further search revealed a black plastic lunchbox sitting on a shelf in the hall closet. Inside was a cellphone and a cube of Styrofoam that was actually two halves taped together. Cody lifted this out and dragged a chair over to the prone man. He sat and got the man's attention.

"What's this?" he asked, waving the cube.

The man reacted in complete terror, recoiling from the thing and making panic sounds behind his gag. Cody pulled it away from the guy and put his hands up, trying to communicate that he had no intention of hurting the man. It did very little to abate the look of utter terror in the guy's eyes.

Cody sighed, put down the Beretta and snapped the tape holding the two sides of the cube together. Cautiously, he lifted the top to expose a test tube. He didn't touch it, but instead lifted the Styrofoam cradle to the light and studied the tube. It was double-sealed with a rubber stopper, two rounds of clear tape and labeled with a bright red biohazard sticker. Based on that and the man's response, he surmised it was some sort of biotoxin, likely scheduled for release in a public place. He resealed the Styrofoam cube and pocketed it and the cellphone. Then he picked up the Beretta and stooped to lift the man from the ground by the elbow.

"Upsy-daisy, pal." Cody wrangled the man to his feet and dragged him across the room to the window. There was a lever on the sill used to rotate open the eight-foot-high glass panel. Fully opened, it allowed just enough room for a man to pass through. Cody forced the man onto the sill. He untied the man's hands and then gestured for him to remove the gag from his own mouth. The man complied.

Four stories below, traffic snarled the narrow boulevard fronting the hotel.

Cody reflected on the poor man's journey. Radicalized by poverty and privation, swept into the White Wolf's fold and then dispatched on this mission, he was nothing more than a pawn in Big Terror's game. Under different circumstances, Cody might actually feel pity for the guy…

But not tonight.

The terrorist's scream echoed all the way down to the street, where he landed on the roof of a parked car, smashing it flat and setting the alarm off. It was still screaming, and a crowd had formed by the time Cody reached the street and vanished into the night.

CHAPTER TWENTY-SEVEN

THE LUSHLY CARPETED and beautifully paneled hallways of Thelma Justice's retreat attested to the woman's enormous wealth. *And horrible taste,* thought Sara as she walked under the watchful eye of Overalls and an armed Fury. There was plenty of artwork – sculptures, paintings, murals – all of them gaudy, with a strange fixation on balloon-ish female butts and breasts. This stuff wasn't Venus on the Half-shell – more like the kind of stuff a pornographic cartoonist might crank out on a drunken bender. It gave the décor the feel of a Roman orgy.

Aisha walked beside her, head down, not subjected to the same level of security but definitely under duress. As they passed through an enclosed atrium, a wide bay window on one side appeared. Beyond lay a vista of snow-capped peaks.

"Very pretty," she remarked.

"We're in the Italian Alps," Aisha said quickly.

"Quiet!" snapped Overalls, shoving Sara roughly enough to cause a stumble.

The atrium became a hallway that ended in a set of double-wide doors. No knock was necessary – the doors parted silently as they approached. *Apparently, we're expected,* Sara thought. Tiff Butler stood waiting in what looked like an ordinary reception area with couches and chairs and a coffee table. Beyond lay the doorway to what looked like an office.

"Hey, girlfriend," Tiff sneered at Sara. "Long time no see."

"Not long enough," Sara growled.

"Oh, now! Don't be like that." Tiff tittered. "Easy come, easy go. We got the drop on you, and *we won.* Don't be a sore loser."

"Give me five minutes alone in a room with you and I'll show you sore," Sara retorted.

"Mm." Tiff's smile widened. "Well, we won't be alone. Some friends of yours are waiting in there. They're very anxious to see you."

Tiff conducted them through the reception area and into the office annex. The place contained cubicles, one large executive desk and an array of computer and audiovisual equipment. Huge flatscreen TVs lined the wall above the desk, at which sat Thelma Justice. Greb Vetrov leaned on the wall behind her.

"Well, well, well," said Thelma Justice. "Look what we've got here, Greb. Seems we've captured ourselves a real, live CIA agent."

"Is not difficult." Vetrov spoke calmly, his eyes heavy-lidded. He looked like he'd been drinking. "CIA's greatest gift to Russia is its incompetence."

"CIA's greatest gift to Russia will be returning you in handcuffs to the Kremlin." Sara's rage surprised even herself. "You miserable son-of-a-bitch! What kind of a man rises to flag rank and then betrays his own country?"

A slow smile spread across Vetrov's face. "What kind of man rises to flag rank at all, hey? Man with balls. With ambition. Such men are not trained dogs who jump through hoops."

"Greb is a very complex man," purred Thelma Justice, casting an admiring glance at her Russian. "Men like him are goal-oriented. They see what they want and they go for it. Such men are not content to remain the servant of others forever."

The simmering rage that had been building inside Sara finally burst out past the dam of her teeth. "There's no higher calling than to be of service," she spat. "To one's family! To one's *country!* That's a sacred trust, given to very few. Anyone who bears that yoke also bears a responsibility to use that power to the benefit of others. Anyone who betrays it harms the innocent, no matter what bullshit, macho fairy tales they tell themselves."

Thelma Justice listened to this impassively. When Sara was done, she offered mocking applause.

"And the award for the biggest patriot goes to Sara Durell." Thelma shook her head. "I wish someone with your passion and intelligence worked for me. You would have risen far in my organization, Sara."

"I'd rather clean toilets."

Thelma shrugged. "That's basically what you *have* been doing, darling. Cleaning the national security toilet that is America's international legacy of repeated failure and brutality. But rejoice, for those days are *over* for you now. Politics are about to change for everybody, forever."

She's delusional, thought Sara. Rich, power-hungry and completely out of her mind, Thelma Justice had hooked up with a man whose appetite for power and control equalled her own. And they were about to do massive damage to the world.

"Your Hummingbird nuclear devices – the portable tactical nukes you had the general steal – have been neutralized, Thelma," she said. "They're buried in the rubble of your mansion in Monte Carlo. Whatever you had planned for them is now canceled."

"We have something more powerful than suitcase nukes," replied Thelma. "More powerful than weapons themselves, which can be lost and replaced. But the item we have at our disposal? It's the kind of thing entire armies – entire *nations* – follow into battle. You see, it's one thing to have the hardware. It's another thing entirely to have a cause."

Thelma jerked her chin and Overalls stepped forward. Grasping Aisha by a shoulder, she guided the girl into the nearest cubicle and sat her in front of the computer terminal there.

"Aisha, tell Sara what you did with the tablet."

The tablet! Sara fought hard to control her emotions. The ancient codex – a clay tablet dating from the First Century which told an alternate version of Genesis and Christ's story – had been at the center of this business from the very beginning. The story of the Messiah and his supposed twin sister Judith whose assistance was required to perform the Gospel's biggest miracles had been a much sought-after treasure throughout the centuries. People had even killed for it. Even people like Vetrov.

Why?

"Cat got your tongue, Aisha?" Thelma held up a hand to restrain Overalls, who seemed keen to beat the answer out of the girl. "Never fear. She already confided in us. The tablet is in a private safety deposit box in her bank in Switzerland. That's where you mailed it in the midst of your adventures in France, isn't it, dear?"

Aisha looked up at Sara, over to Thelma and then back again. Then she dropped her head and nodded miserably.

"And now she is going to arrange its transfer and delivery to us here." Thelma nodded to Overalls, who leaned forward and switched on the computer. "With that in hand, we'll have the raw material to remake the world."

"As *what?*" snarled Sara.

"As a phoenix rising from the ashes." Thelma smiled. "Come on, Sara. Take a look around you. Take a look at what Man – what *men* – have made of this world. Wars, slavery, sexual abuse, destruction of the environment… It's endless! And *always* in the name of knowing what's best for us all. Well, those days are over."

Thelma Justice leaned forward and hit a button on a control panel beside her. Immediately, the huge flat screens jumped to life on the wall behind her. A standard Mercator projection map showing the oceans and continents. Overlaid across it were a series of colored lines moving in a wave-like pattern. Sara recognized these as satellite orbital tracking lines.

"We have the high ground, Sara. We have the ability to unleash the entire spectrum of the US nuclear arsenal however – and on *whomever* – we wish to unleash it. We have the tools, the talent and the advantage." She leaned forward across the desk, a mad smile on her face. "And soon we will have the very item we need to rally the world to our cause after it's all over. We'll offer a new religion, a new Gospel and a new world government. Ruled by those obviously best equipped to handle such a responsibility. *Women.*"

Sara bit her lips, forcing herself not to speak. But thinking: *My God, she's absolutely nuts...*

"Aisha." Thelma raised her chin and glared down at the girl. "Begin the transfer now or Sara dies."

Trembling, Aisha looked up at Sara. A single tear slid down her cheek. Then she turned to the computer keyboard and began typing.

CHAPTER TWENTY-EIGHT

THE TRAIN SLID into the station of the small mountain town just south of Thelma Justice's chateau in the Italian Alps. Cody had taken pains to change his appearance, assuming that the station platform would be monitored by members of Thelma's security team. And so the man who limped off the train bore no resemblance to Jack Cody – or anyone who might pose a threat. Bent-backed, clad in a tweed overcoat and sporting a wispy white beard, he looked every inch the retired university professor his travel documents affirmed him to be, but that just attested to the excellence of Ishigawa's handiwork.

Cody kept up the act through the station concourse to the lobby and the street outside. The streets were quiet, but he detected the tell-tale signs of a town readying itself for its yearly busy season. The mountains in this area were thick with downhill and cross-country ski trails. Soon the winter tourists from the EU would descend with tourist Euros to keep the local economy going. He planned to be long gone by then.

He limped to the nearest cheap bed-and-breakfast place and took a room. Checking his phone, he noted there was still no word from Sara. More determined than ever to recon Thelma Justice's nearby chateau, he readied the materials for his deception.

The Beretta, of course, was crucial. Cody dispensed with his usual shoulder-holster rig in favor of a waist-carry arrangement that operated similarly to a fanny-pack, but instead of a bulge, the hidden pouch held the weapon flush to his body, impossible to detect except during a pat-down. Cody stripped to his shorts and strapped the pouch to his waist, pulling insulated black track pants up over it. Despite the snug fit of the pants, the weapon was all but invisible.

His next crucial component was a backpack – a miracle of CIA innovation that could hold a prodigious amount but which folded up into a square shape about the size of a wallet. The backpack could easily hold the entirety of his professor disguise. He checked and refolded the backpack, stashing it in a back pocket. The final item, a series of lens attachments that could transform his cellphone's camera into a range finder, a thermal imaging sight or night vision rig. These black tubes were laid side-by-side in a flat case similar to that of a minia-ture screwdriver set. He slid that into the pocket beside the folded backpack.

He zipped up the thermal top to the tracksuit, slid his feet into black waterproof sneakers and donned his aging professor costume atop it all. Then, taking up his walking stick, he limped out of the bed-and-breakfast to the street outside.

The helicopter rental firm he had found lay a mile up the street, closer to the "downtown" portion of the small village. Between the bed and breakfast and the rental place lay a small indoor shopping mall – perhaps a half-dozen stores grouped together under one roof with a food court and public rest area. A brisk crowd was moving through the place in the late afternoon. Cody limped to the handicapped washroom, let himself in and locked the door behind him.

Working quickly, he removed his disguise and produced the collapsible backpack. Unfolding it and stowing everything inside took less than two minutes. Then he was emerging, backpack over one shoulder and clad in his black thermal tracksuit, a pair of wraparound shades covering his eyes. Nobody gave him a second glance.

He hiked the mile to the helicopter rental outfit in brisk, lengthy strides. The office itself was a narrow building wedged between two shopfronts. Through the window inset in the door, he could see the place itself consisted of a small waiting area and a single desk and chair occupied by a dark-haired woman of about thirty. Cody knocked. She looked up quickly from her work and then invited him in with a wave of her hand.

"Hi." He allowed himself a nervous-looking grin. "Do you speak English?"

"Of course." She smirked. "English is the international language of aviation, after all. Welcome to Pisa Helicopter Tours. How can I help you today?"

"Great!" Cody set down his backpack and took a seat in one of the guest chairs facing her desk. "My name is Ted Davis. I'm a nature correspondent for Broken Earth magazine. Do you know it?"

"Can't say I do."

"We cover environmental tourism. The effect on ecosystems that results from our carbon and human footprint. It's very popular these days."

"Your magazine or destroying the environment?"

"Touché!"

"We actually get requests for environmental tours regularly here." She held up a brochure. "There are ice fields high in these mountains that have remained unchanged since the dawn of time. Scientists come to study them. And environmental tourists eager to experience the Alps."

"So you've had experience with our readership. That's great! It'll be really helpful, actually."

"Well, I'm glad." She smiled and dragged over a pad and pen. "Are you interested in booking a tour?"

"I am." Reaching into his backpack, he withdrew a large, folded map which he unfurled on her desk. "I've heard about the ice fields. Also about the glacier melt further inland. What I'm hoping is to circle over this valley…here." He pointed. "You know the area?"

"Sure." The woman nodded. "We fly tours there all the time."

"I'd like to book one tomorrow morning."

"Ah. Bad luck." She sat back, crossing her arms. "We're actually closed tomorrow. All our pilots have a day off."

"Damn. That's too bad." He frowned. "I heard a rumor that there's somebody who actually lives up there. Is it true?"

This piqued the woman's interest. "Yes. Have you ever heard of Thelma Justice?"

"The women's rights lady? Sure. Hasn't everybody?" Cody shrugged. "My girlfriend is reading her latest book right now."

"Well, that's her home." The girl extended a hand. "Ted, my name is Giovanna. And I think I may be able to help you after all."

"How?"

"I'll take you myself." She laughed at his surprised expression. "Why, yes. I'm a helicopter pilot, too. I did a tour in the air force. It would be my pleasure to take you on a trip around that area. I'll even be happy to point out Thelma Justice's home to you."

"That would be great," Cody said. And smiled.

CHAPTER TWENTY-NINE

"Excuse me, Mr. President." The chief of staff leaned over and whispered in the president's ear. "We have a Code Tango in the Situation Room, sir."

President Harwood glanced up, nodded and then turned his attention to the group gathered on the couches and seats before of the Oval Office hearth. "Please forgive me, Mr. Prime Minister," he said to the Japanese PM. "I have a situation I must attend to briefly. I'll let the secretary of state take over on my behalf until I return."

The Japanese prime minister nodded and offered a smile of understanding as the president rose and made his way through the chief of staff's office and out into the hall. Enclosed within a bubble of Secret Service agents, he descended the back stairs to the reinforced basement suite that housed the national situation command and control center. From here, POTUS had a full spectrum view of US military and intelligence resources worldwide and access to the latest information regarding threats, domestic or international. Enclosed behind two automated oak doors, the Situation Room itself included an array of computer and audio-visual equipment as well as a large square conference table at which sat representatives of the joint chiefs, general staff and intelligence community. As one, they came to their feet when Harwood entered the room.

"Gentlemen, please take your seats." Harwood settled into a tall-backed chair at the head of the table. "I understand we have a Code Tango?" Under the national security threat-level nomenclature used at the command level, a Code Tango signified a credible terrorist threat against the homeland and/or key allies.

"Yes, sir." The chairman of the joint chiefs stood and approached the large flatscreen monitor mounted on the far wall. As he did, the screensaver dissolved to a black-and-white still photograph of a chaotic street scene: police, ambulance, a crowd gathered around a smashed car. Shrunk down at the edge of the screen were two miniaturized graphics, in position to be enlarged and centered in their turn.

The chief stopped and pointed to the black-and-white image. "This was taken earlier today in Rome. A man jumped from the fourth floor of a hotel – an apparent suicide. Police initiated a standard investigation which revealed that the man was in the country illegally. No passport, no entry visa, no ID to speak of. Police forensics swept his room. I'll let our rep from Fort Detrick take it from here."

The chief nodded to a colonel sitting nearby. He rose, a bald, wiry man wearing round glasses.

"I'm Colonel Glassman, Mr. President. I'm head of the biowarfare research unit at Detrick. Officially, of course, the United States military is a sponsor and signatory of the global ban on biological and chemical weapons." He paused. "Despite this, research continues into development of and counter-measures against such weapons. We were contacted by our colleagues in intelligence when the Italian police discovered CRUMs in the dead man's hotel room."

"Excuse me. Did you say 'crumbs'?" Harwood blinked, puzzled.

"Yes, sir." Glassman approached the flatscreen and enlarged one of the side bar photos. An image of an open black lunchbox on a desk leapt into focus. "The term was developed in a series of high-level meetings we had with our Russian and Chinese counterparts at the end of the Cold War. All parties agreed that bioweapons represented the greatest threat to the major powers. Therefore, the ability to police and control any remaining stockpiles was a priority. And so, we developed the Coded Record for Unlawful Munitions, or CRUM protocol." With the poke of a finger, Colonel Glassman enlarged one corner of the lunchbox. Barely visible were a series of spots which seemed to glow slightly in the light. "In partnership with labs in Moscow and Beijing, we developed the 'glitter' – our nickname of the coded munitions record-tracking system. It's literally a form of radioactive dust that gets sprinkled on shell casings, test tubes and centrifuges containing bio- and chemical-weapons."

"The idea, sir, was that if bioweapons ever appeared on the threat horizon, we could identify where they came from," explained the chairman.

"So, you're telling me these traces positively identify the presence of some sort of bioweapon in this man's hotel room?" Harwood narrowed his eyes. "One that is now missing?"

"Yes, sir." Glassman took up a sheet of paper from the table. "The CRUMs are encoded by munitions type and lot number. This particular set corresponds to a particularly virulent bioweapon developed by the Soviet Union in the late 1980s. It's a variation of smallpox known as *Variola nocturnis*. Night plague. Weaponized versions of a virulent and highly contagious disease for which we have no known cure. Contracting smallpox is a death sentence."

"I have been in contact with my opposite number in the Kremlin," said the Chairman. "He and the Russian president have been extremely forthcoming. They confirm a quantity of the *Variola* plague has gone missing from their storage facility at Pochep. This was the same site from which we believe General Vetrov lifted the suitcase nukes CIA recovered in France."

"Vetrov!" The president's hands fisted. He turned to the CIA director. "Tell me we've got someone on the ground tracking Vetrov and Thelma Justice."

"I've ordered it done, sir," the director sounded tense, unsure.

Harwood's mouth firmed. "And?" he snapped.

"We're in a fog of war, sir." The director's frustration was evident. "I have one of our senior guys, Jared Parnell, working that side of the street. But he seems to have...dropped the ball. We're trying to locate him—"

The president held up a hand. "Parnell. Screwing up. Again."

"Uh, yes sir."

"Mr. Director, this has to stop. Do I make myself clear?"

"Very clear, Mr. President."

"I don't know what Jared Parnell's actual job title is. But I want it changed. Demote the bastard immediately. I don't give a damn where you put him. Have him monitor the parking garage at Langley, for all I care. But

I don't want him anywhere near the line of fire where this is concerned. Is that clear?"

"Perfectly, sir." The director held up a card. "One piece of info, sir. We believe the dead man may have entered the country via a phoney international courier service called Tellerman. Our initial investigations indicate the front was set up by Thelma Justice and her organization. Sir…" he hesitated, "our records indicate Tellerman sent flights to fifty major world capitals. Since then, they've gone dark."

"Alright." Harwood pushed back from the table. "Mr. Director, I want our allies in Five Eyes informed. Activate your special operations team and notify section heads in all fifty cities. I'll need hourly updates."

"Yes, sir."

Harwood rose and left the room, attended by his Service detail and chief of staff. He drew the latter to him and spoke confidentially. "Get that retired British spy in Moscow on the phone. We'll use him and his network. I need answers. And I need them fast. Get on it."

"Yes, Mr. President."

CHAPTER THIRTY

"ON YOUR FEET." Overalls glared at Sara from the doorway of the "cell" she shared with Aisha. "She wants to see you. *Both* of you."

Sara sighed and rose from the couch. Their "cell" actually resembled a pair of adjoining rooms in an upscale hotel. But the reality of their confinement was beyond doubt. As they stepped from the room into the hallway, Sara noted the two Furies posted there holding machine pistols. *No way out*, Sara realized. The window of their room let out onto a sheer vertical drop of over 1000 feet. And if they tried the hall, they would be shredded by weapons fire.

Overalls led them through the same atrium. But instead of turning into the office complex, she opened a second door further down the hall. It led into a darkened, comfortable sitting area warmed by a large stone hearth before which was a padded sectional couch. Thelma Justice sat there, studying the contents of a folder. She looked up when Overalls entered.

"Ah! Here they are." She beamed a magnanimous

smile. Sara could not shake the feeling that something was up. "Do come in, ladies. Please have a seat. Would you care for some coffee?" Thelma gestured toward a tea service on the coffee table. "Or perhaps some juice or a soft drink? I'd like us to be comfortable while we talk."

"Nothing for me," said Sara. Aisha shook her head, too.

"Very well." Thelma poured herself a cup of coffee and waited until everyone was seated before starting.

"As you can imagine, I'm quite busy." She smiled. "We have a lot on the go, do Greb and I. But I wanted to give you the opportunity to listen and understand what I'm trying to do. Because I can't help feeling that, as fellow women, you might understand. For example, the oppression that we deal with as a sex."

Sara groaned and rolled her eyes. "You've brought us here to your million-dollar chateau in the Italian Alps to talk about how you're oppressed?"

"*All* women are oppressed, Sara," said Thelma. "Look at you in the CIA. How many women are in senior positions of leadership?"

"Plenty," countered Sara. "And the women who are there are stone professionals who have proven their loyalty and efficacy through years of sacrifice and service. Not because they ticked off some boxes on some affirmative action checklist."

"Mm." Thelma turned to Aisha. "And, you? A young woman of your obvious gifts and talents. Why should your brother Achmed and not you be taking over the kingdom?"

"Because Achmed is older," said Aisha. "He is first born son. The throne is his right."

"See? There you go." Thelma flapped a hand. "His 'right'. And why is that? Centuries of patriarchal oppression reinforced through religion. That is why your tablet – the relic you've arranged to transfer to us here – is so important."

"Explain," said Sara.

"Oh, I would think that would be obvious." Thelma's eyelids dropped to half-mast. "Look at the Old Testament, the Q'uran and the Gospels. In the first two, you have the all-knowing sky-father. The thunder god who imparts wisdom and punishment. And in Jesus you have confirmation – of maleness, of male domination of the spiritual and moral realms. Why do you think there is a *male* priesthood in Islam and the majority of Christian denominations? It's the same old game. Male soldiers backed up by male priests backed up by a great, big, dick-swinging male God. *That's* the justification."

"But what if we could change that?"

Sara shook her head. "Change their conception of God? So their conception of everything else changes along with it?"

"The tablet – along with its story of a Jesus who performed miracles with the help of His twin sister – will allow us to do that." Thelma smiled.

"Great," Sara groaned. "A nice loving mommy-god, rising from the ashes of a nuclear holocaust to re-civilize the world. Something like that?"

"Something like that. First, the shock and awe. Then the healing." Thelma looked up when Overalls opened the door, standing aside to usher someone into the room. "I gave instructions we were not to be interrupted."

"I'm sorry, ma'am. But this gentleman—"

At this, the White Wolf burst past Overalls and entered, a tornado of angry energy. He stomped over to Thelma and planted himself before her.

"There is a problem." He turned to glance at Thelma's two guests. "We received—" Seeing Aisha, he paused. "Why, Princess," a mocking smile played about his lips, "a pleasure to make the acquaintance of the sheikh's daughter."

"A pleasure to make the acquaintance of the man who murdered my uncle Fahd," she replied coolly. "The enemy of my family is my enemy."

"Pfft." The White Wolf gave a disdainful wave and turned to Thelma. "We have encountered a problem."

"Speak freely, my friend." Thelma shrugged. "There is nothing you can say here that will leave this room. Our plans are underway. Nothing can stop them now."

The White Wolf's mouth firmed, and he looked from Sara to Aisha and back again before answering Thelma.

"Our operative in Rome," he said. "Met with an unfortunate accident. He was pushed from his hotel room window and his sample was taken."

Thelma frowned.

Aisha looked down.

And Sara grinned. *Cody,* she thought. And her smile broadened.

CHAPTER THIRTY-ONE

THE NEXT MORNING, Cody followed the same routine to leave the bed and breakfast, hobbling out on his cane to the handicapped washroom at the mall to doff his old man disguise and re-emerge in his insulated black tracksuit and shades, the backpack over his shoulder. There was a taxi stand just up the street with three cars waiting. Cody got into the first one and gave the driver the directions Giovanna had provided to the chopper pad. It was a short journey out of town up the highway to an access road which led across cow pastures to the small air station. The tiny airfield was dedicated to the chopper tours; Cody saw three helicopters emblazoned with the Pisa Tours logo. Even from a distance, it was obvious the place was closed. Nevertheless, Giovanna stood waiting by the gate in the low fence surrounding the helipad, her dark hair billowing in the wind.

She's an attractive woman, Cody thought, flicking surreptitious glances at her while he paid the cabbie. He doubted all Italian army chopper pilots were so attractive.

"So, Ted," she said with a smile as he approached, "you ready to do some flying?"

"Sure am." He smiled in what he hoped looked like nervousness.

"Ever been in a helicopter before?" She unlatched the gate and led him to the nearest chopper.

"Once," Cody lied. "Broken Earth sent me on assignment to cover the impact of eco-tourism on Angel Falls in Venezuela. You know it? It's the tallest waterfall in the world. They sent me in onboard a helicopter. I, uh, used up a lot of barf bags…" He grimaced, pretending to be ashamed.

"Ha ha. You won't have that problem here, Ted," she assured him. "Places like Venezuela are warm weather systems, which means a lot of turbulence and instability. It's different here in the Alps. Colder, sure. But the air is much calmer. You'll have a nice smooth ride. You'll see."

The chopper was an NH 500, a civilian version of an Italian military transport helicopter. Generally used for ferrying personnel, it resembled one of the old-style passenger Hueys, with its lozenge-shaped fuselage. The ship was set up to comfortably accommodate four passengers, including the pilot. Giovanna held open the passenger door for Cody and leaned in to help him as he pretended to fumble with his harness. "Allow me," she said with a gallant smile. Cody permitted her to lean in over him to fasten the snaps.

She ran through her pre-flight checks swiftly, her military background obvious in her clear-crisp movements. As Cody fumbled out camera equipment, Giovanna made final preparations and got the rotors spinning. Within a few minutes, they were airborne.

"Have you had experience with glaciers before, Ted? With icefields?"

"A little," he said. "We did a photoshoot in Banff a few years ago. Went back last year. The glacier has really shrunk. Global warming."

"So, you're a believer in climate change." Through the radio headset, Giovanna's voice swelled with satisfaction. "I am very glad to hear that. Not surprising given the magazine you work for. But I find it rare in men."

"Oh?"

"Mm. Concern for the environment, protection of fragile ecosystems, awareness of the future... These are things that women attend to naturally. It's part of our nurturing nature. Developed over time as a result of our focus on children."

"Sure thing."

"It makes us more empathetic. More attuned and caring." She flashed him a sidelong glance. "Are you a feminist?"

"Certainly," Cody lied. He wasn't. He was a humanist. But he understood the political overlap of feminism and environmentalism and played to that in his current cover. "It's time for, uh, women to assume a greater share of the burden in wielding political power."

He saw a smile play about her lips. *Home run,* he thought. It seemed he had lucked out and found Pisa Tours' environmental activist pilot.

They swept out over the vista of mismatched peaks and jagged, stone-strewn valleys. From high above, tiny ribbons of grey wrapped the circumferences of mountains. *Highways,* he thought. There were roads through this region, but they were mostly high and impassable in hard weather. If Thelma Justice had selected the locale for privacy, she couldn't have chosen much better.

He pointed the camera and snapped a few pictures.

"Beautiful country," he said. "This must be incredibly

difficult terrain for your military to defend."

She shrugged. "We do well enough. We routinely train with our Swiss partners in securing and protecting these regions."

"Well, it can't be easy. And you said people actually live out here?"

There was a long pause before she answered. Cody looked over to find her studying him.

"One person," she said quietly. "That I know of. You mentioned her before."

"I did?"

"Thelma Justice."

"Oooh. Right. The female empowerment lady." He nodded. "When we were chatting in the office."

"You don't recall?"

"I didn't until just now." He swallowed. Something between them had shifted and didn't feel right.

"You have to understand, Ted. Thelma Justice has done great things for women." Giovanna's jaw firmed as she adjusted the pitch and switched course. "She is someone whom we all admire. Without Thelma, where would the modern women's rights movement be?"

"Well, yeah. Sure…"

"We have to be careful, Ted. Thelma has to be protected. There are people – *men* – who want to harm her."

"That's terrible!"

"But what they don't understand is that the women who followed Thelma are ready to do anything for her. And we are everywhere."

Below, the contours of Thelma's chateau appeared out of the mist. The helicopter began descending toward it.

Oh, shit, he thought.

CHAPTER THIRTY-TWO

OVERALLS ENTERED their rooms again shortly after their return. Thelma was calling for another meeting.

"Not you," snapped Overalls as Sara rose to join Aisha. She began to protest but Aisha raised her hand.

"I'll be alright, Sara," she said quietly. "Just wait here for me."

Sara's jaw firmed. But she nodded and acquiesced.

During the trip down the opulent, tasteless hallways, Aisha focused on her breathing. Deep, calming breaths from her diaphragm helped regulate her mind and heartbeat. She would need all of her inner resources intact if she were to face Thelma alone.

This time, the office annex was occupied. In addition to Thelma seated at her desk below the row of flatscreens, there was a scattering of technicians, perhaps four or five. They moved from cubicle to cubicle, attending to workstations on which were displayed smaller versions of the satellite tracking picture above. Again and again, they returned to hover over one man in particular – a chubby, balding guy with glasses who sat in the cubicle nearest to

Thelma. Aisha guessed this must be the famous Dr. Nodwell, late of the US defense establishment.

"Ah, Your Royal Highness." Thelma looked up with a kindly expression on her face. From her place beside Thelma, Tiff Butler smiled, too. The reporter seemed to have taken on the role of flunkey since arriving. "Please have a seat. How are your accommodations?"

"Claustrophobic." Aisha smiled and settled into the padded guest chair immediately to the left of the desk. She suppressed a smile of amusement as Thelma and Tiff shared a look.

"Princess, I wanted to speak to you personally." Thelma swiveled and sat back in her executive chair, lacing her fingers atop her head and studying Aisha frankly. "The last time we spoke, Sara Durell was with us. I understand the attachment and loyalty you must feel to the woman who has protected you these past few days. But remember that she *is* the servant of a foreign government."

"An *ally,*" Aisha corrected her. "An allied government. My father the sheikh has enjoyed excellent relations with every president since Lyndon Johnson. We hold the Americans in great esteem in our country."

"Of course, I understand the need for diplomacy," said Thelma. "Please don't forget that the Order of World Harmony is a global organization. I, too, enjoy relationships with world leaders."

"I see. Does the president regularly call you for advice on Middle Eastern diplomacy? Because President Harwood and my father speak almost monthly."

Again, the shared look between Tiff and Thelma.

"So, you haven't heard." Thelma's hands dropped to the arms of her chair and her eyes narrowed. "I suppose you *have* been…indisposed…"

Aisha gripped the arms of her chair. "What?"

"Aisha, your father has died." Tiff Butler pushed a copy of USA Today across the desk towards her. "Your brother Achmed is now the sheikh." As an afterthought, she added: "I'm so sorry."

The bold headline read:

ROYAL U.S. ALLY DIES AFTER LENGTHY ILLNESS

Aisha drew a deep breath, looked down at the carpet and stilled the shrieking grief that rose like a tornado in her chest. The news had been expected; her father had been dying for months. Still. The actuality of the event hit her like a falling piano.

She remembered her dignity. She was still a princess.

"Peace be upon him," she said quietly. And settled her eyes on Thelma Justice, her face as hard as a poker shark's. She would give this mad, infidel woman no entry, no emotional lever with which to control her.

Nothing.

"Aisha, I'm so sorry." Thelma leaned forward, elbows on her knees, an expression of sympathy on her face. "I can imagine how, at a time like this, it helps to have friends. I would like to be your friend. And I would very much like you to be mine. And so, I would like you to understand what we're trying to do here."

"I think I understand well enough."

"Do you?" Thelma Justice frowned and sat back, bringing her hands together on the desk in front of her. "Do you really? Perhaps, isolated in your wealth and privilege, you fail to understand the pressing need to change our world. It's gone on as it has for far too long. The poverty, injustice and suffering that men – that Man

– has inflicted on the Earth has been massive. And it's unsustainable. We have to stop the suffering. We have to bind the wounds of the world. We must lead with love."

"Love?"

Aisha's voice, normally soft, cracked in the room like a whip, silencing the buzzing technicians and drawing all eyes forward to where she sat, arms gripping the chair, quivering with rage.

"What do you know about *love*, you sick psychopath?" Aisha blazed with rage as she glared across the desk at Thelma. "Stop the suffering? Bind the wounds? *How?* By inflicting a massive global disaster that will kill hundreds of millions and unleash untold suffering on the survivors? Mass murder on a scale the likes of Hitler and Stalin could only dream of? You claim to be some sort of world teacher. Some guru or avatar that has the answers to lead us into a bold new age. But you don't. And you *aren't*. You're just a power-hungry lunatic who wants to murder people. You offer me friendship out of a false sense of caring? No thank you. I have a family and a kingdom full of subjects who love me and my family. They love us because we would do anything to make their lives better. My father died in service to his kingdom, and my brother and I would gladly lay down our lives for our subjects. You have nothing – *nothing* – to offer me but lies! And your nonsense dreams of global domination. You're disgusting. And deluded. And you make me sick."

Thelma Justice listened impassively as Aisha finished. The girl glared at her with such raw anger that it singed the air between them.

"I see you remain unconvinced by my arguments about love," said Thelma. She shrugged. "Perhaps a different argument will convince you."

And before Aisha could react, Thelma surged from her chair and seized Tiff Butler by the throat. The journalist's eyes bugged, and her surprise was great enough to allow Thelma to unbalance and bend her backwards across the edge of the desk. Thelma clambered onto Tiff, straddling her as her fingers tightened around the thrashing woman's throat. After a minute, the thrashing limbs stilled, and Tiff Butler died with a gurgle.

"Love is organic, Princess," said Thelma, climbing down off of the body and wiping her hands on her skirt. "And like any organic entity, it requires sustenance. That means *sacrifice*. One thing devouring another to keep the circle of life nourished. Don't feel bad for Tiff Butler. She was a withered branch that needed pruning. Likewise, we will prune and nourish the Earth."

She frowned reflectively as two Furies rushed in to collect and remove Tiff's corpse.

"Perhaps you'll understand that someday." Thelma smiled. "You may go."

CHAPTER THIRTY-THREE

"WHAT ARE YOU DOING?"

Giovanna, the former Italian military chopper pilot, did not respond but focused on guiding the chopper down toward the chateau. Cody had walked right into a trap.

His options were nonexistent. Even if he attacked and managed to wrestle the control stick away from Giovanna, he still couldn't fly a helicopter. And the likelihood that his action would cause the two of them to crash was inevitable. He had no choice but to wait for the chopper to land.

She's one of theirs, he thought. *Once we land, I'll grab her and use her as a bargaining chip...*

A light snow had begun falling – flakes twisting on the wind, falling to melt on the stones below. There was no landing pad to speak of – just a wide stone balcony big enough to hold a football game. As they descended, the figures below resolved into visibility: two armed Furies and a bald, black woman wearing overalls. When they were a dozen feet from touchdown, the woman in overalls gestured and the Furies trained their rifles on the cockpit windshield. The message was plain.

If I grab her, we both die, he realized. And fought the anger rising inside him.

He was trapped.

With a bump, they landed. Seconds later, the woman in overalls was rushing to the passenger door, one of the Furies behind her, rifle raised. She yanked open the door and gestured for Cody to exit…or else.

Giovanna turned to him with a smile. "Thank you for flying with Pisa Helicopter Tours," she said.

Glaring at her, he unclipped the seat harness and exited the chopper, hands high. The woman in overalls gave him a quick pat-down, found the Beretta and assorted gear and confiscated the lot. Then she grabbed him by the scruff of the neck and began pushing him toward an open doorway, the Furies following, guns on him.

"You just make a move," she hissed. "Go on and do it, mister man. These two sisters will blow you to kingdom come."

Cody did the exact opposite. His training on capture and interrogation demanded a 'soft-but-flexible' approach to dealing with captors. The trick was to think long-game. His job right now was to conserve energy and plan in advance which hills he would plant his flag on. He recalled Commander Murphy of SEAL Team Two, who had led the course.

"Resistance should be targeted," Murphy had said. *"If they want you to go into a room, go. Let your body go limp and offer them no excuse to escalate to physical torture. That will come anyway. You want to have the gumption and energy in reserve to stonewall where and when it matters."*

Murphy had been an absolute bear of an instructor.

Captured during the Gulf War, he had endured two weeks of torture before his team-mates swooped in to get him. The man had forgotten more about survival, evasion, resistance and escape than most people would ever know. Cody's capture was disaster writ large. He represented a windfall for Thelma Justice and Vetrov – a trained, active-duty US counter-intel operative with a wealth of information on clandestine weapons and tactics. They could break him. Or sell him to the highest bidder.

"Psychological warfare works both ways," Murphy's voice continued in his mind. *"Preparing the moves and the mind-games you plan to pull on them will occupy your mind. Keep you from spiraling."*

"Spiraling." That was the term. *Fear leads to impulsive decision-making,* Cody remembered. *Impulsiveness leads to bad judgment, which leads to mistakes, which leads to despair. And despair is deadly.*

They were through the door now. Cody was being pushed down a narrow stone hallway that ended in a carpeted stairway.

"Breadcrumbs," had been Murphy's major point. *"Plan a path of false data that you can parcel out piece-by-piece. Lead them down the garden path to someplace of no value to them. Offer minimal resistance. Crack easily for the first piece of data, then resist a bit. Make them believe you are hiding something valuable."*

Cody began planning his path of crumbs. Meanwhile, they were bringing him up the stairs in a seriously professional fashion. One Fury was climbing up ahead of him backwards, the rifle leveled at his face. The woman in overalls was one step below, but slightly to one side. And the second Fury was close behind.

No way out…

The stairs topped out onto a narrow landing facing a secure steel fire door. While the Furies watched him, Overalls unlocked the door and pushed him through. He entered a small, hexagonal sitting room that looked like something from a luxury hotel. No sooner had he been deposited inside than the Furies and their boss in overalls were retreating, guns up, securing the door behind them.

"Cody?"

He turned. Aisha and Sara had entered the room through another door. Despite their circumstances, a wave of relief washed over him.

"Hey there." He grinned. "Did you guys miss me?"

CHAPTER THIRTY-FOUR

DR. CLARENCE NODWELL, formerly of MIT and of JPL, former advisor to the Oval Office and US Strategic Space Command, creator of RaptorNet, sat in his cubicle and marveled in disbelief at the array of thermonuclear power at his disposal from his laptop fire-control board.

Now I am become Shiva, he thought. *Destroyer of worlds ...*

The US nuclear deterrent is the largest of its kind ever developed in the history of modern warfare. The full spectrum arsenal, or 'Triad' as it's designated in operational terms, comprises an array of land-based nuclear missiles, sub-based ICBMs and strategic aircraft packed with nuclear ordnance – almost 4,000 nuclear weapons in total, capable of delivering billions of kilotons of damage. All of it controlled by RaptorNet. And RaptorNet was controlled by him.

Not really me, thought Nodwell, glancing up at Thelma Justice where she sat at the head of the room. *Her.*

His wife Irma had been the first to fall under Thelma's spell. Being a fellow of JPL afforded Nodwell with various gratuities, among which appeared one day a set of tickets to the taping of a 'live' broadcast special featuring Thelma Justice. Nodwell had stayed home, close to solving an equation for calibrating blast yields, and Irma had gone with her best girlfriend Sadie. She had not returned home for three days afterwards. And when she did, she was a changed person.

Nodwell shot Thelma Justice a sour look before returning his attention to the scrolling stream of data that was the designated target uploads, newly programmed into the RaptorNet matrix by himself on behalf of the Order of Universal Harmony.

When asked where she'd been, Irma told him she had gone for a three-day 'cleanse' at a women's ranch in the foothills. Sacred land: no man had ever set foot there, she claimed. There she had been exposed to the teachings of Thelma Justice, experienced colonic irrigation and her first lesbian encounter. At Nodwell's objection to this, she'd raised a hand.

"Sadie and I are a couple now," she said. "You can accept an open marriage or lose half of everything you own, and the other half in court battling the Order of World Harmony, which will cover our legal fees."

Reluctantly, he'd caved to the deal. Sadie moved in. He got booted from his bedroom so took to sleeping on his couch in the office to avoid the bed-jangling racket they made each night. His work on the blast yield equation continued. And Irma's indoctrination deepened.

He had been surprised, upon reaching the upper levels of academia and government, to learn how small the world of national military and scientific policy actually was. Irma and Sadie sailed out among the social set of the military-industrial intelligentsia, recruiting more wives and female scientists to Thelma Justice's cause. And one day he had emerged from another night in his basement office to learn that the Order of World Harmony now owned his house.

When he stormily confronted Irma and Sadie about this in their old bedroom, he was intercepted by a large bald black woman in overalls who told him to simmer down or leave.

"Dr. Nodwell," Thelma Justice was speaking now, "at what stage of your procedures tonight would you say RaptorNet will be fully under our control?"

"One...sec." Nodwell brought up a calculator on his computer desktop. "Well, we're just finishing uploading your launch sequences now, Ms. Justice. I would say we're about seventy percent of the way toward having absolute control right now. But full control? We're probably looking at another hour. By then we'll be so far into ninety percent territory, it won't make much difference anyway."

"General Vetrov helped secure a portion of the information needed to completely compromise the system, correct?"

"Yes, ma'am. He did."

"Is General Vetrov's contribution to the project more or less complete?"

Nodwell considered the question. "I'd say so, yes, ma'am," he said finally.

She returned her attention to the file on the desk before her. Nodwell went back to stewing about the past.

Irma had signed over everything to the organization: the car, the house, even their stock portfolio. In exchange, she was now a 'protectorate' of the Order – a sort of living ATM, whose job it was to maintain a simulacrum of their former life while channeling everything to The Cause. Nodwell, semi-retired, had outlived his usefulness as a competitive wage-earner in the upper echelons of US defense policy, so traded on his classified knowledge.

He handed over RaptorNet for the right to remain in his own house and continue his own research. He hadn't been stupid. He had begun plotting an escape, a way out. But just as he had begun taking the first concrete steps to achieving that goal, Irma had informed him he was being transferred to TJ's mountain fortress in the Alps. She and Sadie were going to the Bahamas.

"What about our marriage?"

"Already annulled." She'd placed the legal documents on the table. He awoke the next morning to find her gone and an armed escort waiting at the door. They flew him here, placed him in a windowless cell for sixteen hours per day and allowed him to work, trading RaptorNet for the right to survive.

He was Thelma Justice's trained attack dog, guarding an array of nuclear tripwires. Soon, he knew, she planned to pluck a vast melody on a lyre strung with those wires. How had he gotten himself here?

By being a coward. By going along to get along. By being the spineless cuckold to his wife's lesbian adventures. He should have stood his ground. He should have put his foot down. But, instead, he had simply gone along and hoped the better angels of people's nature would prevail. And now that they hadn't, he no longer cared. To hell with the world, and everyone in it,

A bell chimed on his desktop.

"We have reached systems nominal status, Ms. Justice," he said. "Full control shortly. We'll soon have complete access across the triad."

"Very well. Set for maximum destruction and begin countdown."

"Yes, Ms. Justice."

This is the way the world ends, thought Nodwell, entering the target telemetry. *Not with a bang, but an equation.*

CHAPTER THIRTY-FIVE

TURNED out Cody was as eager to hear their information as they were to hear his. Between the three of them, they were more or less able to piece together the entirety of the plan engineered by Thelma Justice, Vetrov and the White Wolf. Cody explained the circumstances surrounding his acquisition of the vial marked with the biohazard sticker. Sara told him what she had learned from listening to Thelma Justice.

"They seem to be planning a two-pronged assault," she concluded. "They'll unleash whatever they want from the US nuclear arsenal via RaptorNet and follow it up with a bioweapons attack on the ground. The two crises will combine to completely destabilize western civilization as we know it."

"And Thelma Justice will step in to restore order," Cody finished for her. "It's the classic megalomaniac's fantasy. Remake the world in your own image. Exercise complete control. Warlord of a post-apocalyptic kingdom."

He paused on a long note of awkward silence. Everyone waited. Then Aisha spoke.

"I'm sorry," she said simply. "Sara, Jack…I'm so sorry. I made the mistake I made for the best of intentions. But it still turned out to be a terrible error. And I brought hardship and suffering on you both. I'm sorry. I should have trusted you. I don't know what else to say."

Sara hesitated. Part of her was still furious with the girl for running out on them and landing them here. But part of her also understood. Once upon a time she had been young and confused. But her confusion had driven her onto the path of convention and conformity: she had followed her predecessors into the military, and then government service. It was a similar impulse that drove military families to send generation after generation into uniform.

And what does a girl like Aisha have for a role model, for a precedent? Nothing traditional. Muslim society wasn't well known for its female heroes. She turned to Cody.

He remained where he was, squatting on his haunches, thinking. When he spoke, it wasn't directly to her apology, but obviously about it.

"We always make mistakes when we're young," he said slowly. "In my experience, the people who make the biggest mistakes tend to learn the most. You have a huge responsibility awaiting you in adult life. Now is a good time to learn this lesson." He fixed her with a serious stare. "I would rather this kill me or Sara than harm a nation full of people. That's what you'll be responsible for."

Aisha was chewing over these words when the door swung open. Thelma Justice and Vetrov entered, covered by Overalls. The bald woman wore Cody's Beretta and an Uzi submachine pistol on a strap over her shoulder, gripping the weapon carelessly in slack hands as she studied Cody with dumb belligerence.

"And so our story ends," Thelma Justice hummed. "Sara Durell, Jack Cody and Princess Aisha – the three persons who posed the greatest threat to our project's success will be here to watch it flower into bloom. It's amazing, isn't it? Watching the Age of Justice emerge?"

"Age of Justice." Sara smirked. "Kind of has a narcissistic ring to it, don't you think?"

"Because *my* name is Justice?" Thelma smiled nastily. "Oh, no. It will be the Age of Justice because, for the first time, true justice – *real* justice, justice from a humanistic, female perspective – will be imposed."

"And who decides what's just?" asked the princess angrily. "We live in a world of competing religions and political ideologies. One's justice is another's heresy. Diplomatic and legal norms have been set – by the UN, by the International Criminal Court. Why overthrow all of that? How will you mediate between competing interests?"

"By eliminating them, of course!" Thelma Justice's expression was one of complete surprise, as if shocked her solution wasn't obvious to all. "Destroy anyone and everyone that doesn't agree with us. That way, there will be no competing ideologies to consider or poison the minds of our followers. Only that of the Grand Matriarch, ruler of civilization."

A knock came on the door behind them. Overalls backed toward it, keeping the Uzi trained on Cody and Sara. She opened the door one-handed to reveal Nodwell standing there.

"Ms. Justice, you asked to be informed when we

achieved one hundred percent mastery over RaptorNet. That time has come. We now own the entire triad."

Vetrov beamed, a smile on his face so bright it dimmed the rest of the room. At last! He had wrested the sword of his most powerful and hated enemy from its grasp. Now all that remained was to turn it against itself. He rotated toward Thelma Justice, anticipating a return smile, only to be shocked by the barrel of the little silver revolver that fired point-blank into the center of his forehead.

Vetrov went stiff and collapsed like a ragdoll. Because of the angle of the shot and the positions of everyone in the room, the gore from Vetrov's skull had exploded backwards, the edge of the geyser spraying one side of Sara's face in a mist of red dots.

Cody registered the eruption of Vetrov's skull and contents, grimaced and looked away.

Princess Aisha blanched, turned a shade of green and vomited.

Only Sara, spotted in gore, did not flinch. She did not react with even the slightest twinge of fear or retreat from the nightmare mess that enveloped her, pieces of which had once been the skull and brains of her most dreaded adversary.

"With complete ownership of RaptorNet, Greb Vetrov's part in the grand design has been achieved. Thank you, Dr. Nodwell, for informing me." Thelma Justice nodded to the man before holstering her nickel-plated revolver and gazing down on Vetrov's body. "Let us now pause in remembrance of the dead."

She bowed her head.

"Completely out of her mind," muttered Cody.

CHAPTER THIRTY-SIX

THE CALL to prayer echoed across the Athens skyline. It could have been a scene from the future – the ultra-modern horizon of steel and glass as backdrop to the voice of the *muezzin* proclaiming the *adhān,* the time for daily prayer in a city fully and finally under occupation by the Caliphate...

But it was not. Not today, at any rate. For the skyline itself was being viewed through the glass window of an eighth-floor hotel room, and the voice of the *muezzin* himself was not an echo but instead a broadcast over one of the Islamic radio stations at the far end of Greek FM radio dial. It was a scene perfect for an audience of one – the man who stood at the window.

His orange jumpsuit hanging in the closet behind him, Ibrahim Fata, the first of the fifty men deposited by Tellerman Courier Service jet in a global capital, began this day as he had each day for the past week – by rising early and washing, straightening up his room, unrolling the towel he had adapted for use as a prayer mat and checking the clock. Once the *muezzin's* call was finished, he would pray and then exercise for an hour or two – push-ups, sit-ups, squats and isometrics. By the time he finished, the first of his two daily meals would arrive, and he would take time to savor an enjoyable breakfast.

Ibrahim Fata could neither read nor write. If he could, he might have requested a copy of the Q'uran to supplement what he recognized as a Bible in the bedside table drawer. But upon reflection, he gave thanks to Allah he never learned to read because such a request might have aroused suspicions among the infidels of this city. So he spent the time between breakfast and the noon prayer watching television, trying to pick up some Greek phrases and expressions. So far, he had memorized a dozen or so.

The call of the *muezzin* faded, and Ibrahim presented himself at the foot of his ad-hoc "prayer rug", his mind focused on the light breaking on the south-eastern horizon. He was about to begin when a rustling sound from behind distracted his attention. He turned in time to see a sheet of paper pushed under his hotel room door.

Ibrahim waited for the paper to stop moving. Then he drew a deep breath, made a decision and disengaged from prayer to step over and pick up the paper. Moving into the bathroom, he closed the door, switched on the light and studied the page. Drawn in blue ballpoint pen were a series of shapes and lines that it took him a moment to recognize as a representation of streets and buildings. Someone had drawn him a map, with a circled red 'X' marking the hotel where he stood and an arrow demonstrating a route he was to follow. He resolved to study the diagram after prayer when the cell-phone rang.

Breath caught in his throat.

"The phone is set to receive calls only. You cannot call

from the phone. Keep the phone by your side at all times. Answer immediately when it rings..."

He folded the paper and put it in his pocket. Then, moving quickly, he crossed the space between the bathroom and the closet and took down the black lunchbox from its shelf. Bringing it into the bathroom and closing the door behind him, he opened the lunchbox. The phone chimed a third time. He unfolded and answered it.

"Salaam aleikum."

"Aleikum-al-salaam, Ibrahim." He recognized the voice of Mustafa, the White Wolf's aide-de-camp. "Greetings. Are you ready?"

"I am ready, in the name of Allah, the compassionate and merciful."

"Ameen. Good. You have received the map?"

"I have. Yes." He drew it out of his pocket and unfolded it. "I recognize the shape of the hotel and the street outside."

"Good. Your time is coming, my friend." Mustafa paused and seemed to rearrange some papers at the other end of the line. "Notice the arrow. That is the route you will follow. You will exit the hotel, make a left and then walk four blocks before making another left. You will walk two more blocks until coming to a fence."

"Naeam, sayidi. Yes, sir."

"You will find the fence cut in a triangular pattern. You will lift it and go through. You will follow the hill to the paved road, and the paved road down to the aquifer. It resembles a pond."

"Naeam, sayidi."

"When you reach the pond, you will open the white cube we gave you. Inside is a glass tube with a stopper on top. The stopper is taped into place with very strong tape. Hold back the knife from tonight's dinner. You will need it in the morning."

"Naeam, sayidi."

"Remove the glass vial. Cut off the tape and pull out the stopper. Pour the contents of the vial into the man-made pond there. Then smash the glass and throw the pieces into the pond, as well."

"Naeam, sayidi."

"You will die shortly afterwards." Mustafa paused. "Your death will be to the glory of our cause. Today is your last full day on Earth. Spend it preparing to enter Paradise."

"Naeam, sayidi."

"Salaam-aleikum."

"Aleikum al-salaam."

Mustafa hung up.

Ibrahim hung up and closed the cellphone, replacing it inside the black lunchbox. Then he took out the Styrofoam square, slit the tape holding the cube together and pulled it apart.

There inside was the glass vial, stoppered and sealed by red tape. Ibrahim reminded himself to keep back the knife from tonight's dinner as he had been instructed to do.

Today is your last full day on Earth.

He resealed the cube, replaced it in the lunchbox and sealed it. Then he replaced it on the closet shelf before returning to the towel he had laid out for its specific use.

Morning had come.

It was time to pray.

CHAPTER THIRTY-SEVEN

THELMA JUSTICE, arms folded in satisfaction, stood examining the satellite display on the huge flatscreen at the front of her control-room. In amongst the dozen or so broken, pale white lines were four bold ones: red, yellow, blue and green. Although each line represented a satellite, these brightly colored solids represented birds of special importance. They denoted the four "queens", or master control satellites that brokered and shunted signals between the rest. The queens were fundamental to RaptorNet's entire operation. The irony of their nomenclature was not lost on her.

"Blue Queen transiting at juncture Sierra-Mike," said Nodwell from his desk, his voice magnified over the control-room PA. "Exiting EUCOM. Entering CENTCOM."

"So there's no chance of any of this is being picked up at the Pentagon?" she asked. "No chance any of this is being noted as unusual?"

"No, ma'am," replied Nodwell, cupping his mike. "All of this is routine. I've scripted the satellite navigational plan to be driven off of a 'black box' software engine. According to the Pentagon specs, the black box is a random algorithm generator. But I've built a backdoor into it that I control."

"How?" She narrowed her eyes at him.

"It's a series of trigonometry equations." Nodwell's voice was calm even as sweat beaded his wrists and brow. He had seen what she had done to Tiff Butler and Vetrov. He wanted to solidify his status as invaluable. "They're sequenced but…randomly. I did that to avoid anyone hacking in and just solving the equations. There are variables which…"

"Fine, fine." She flapped a hand. "So you go in through your back door? Adjust the equations? And then…?"

"And then we do whatever you want, Ms. Justice," he said quietly. "Keep a low profile. Hijack the system openly. Or just starting firing nukes."

"Alright." She picked some lint off her sleeve. "Go ahead and bring up the target projection package."

"Will do…"

The satellite projection lines faded from the Mercator projection of the Earth's surface. In their place, a series of red mushroom clouds appeared, each one rippling with menace like an animated demon. The 'clouds' were evenly distributed across the continents.

"Let's run through the sequence again," she ordered.

"Yes, ma'am." Nodwell toggled some buttons on his keyboard. "Once we reach J-hour, my subroutines will be implemented through the black box. This will have the effect of locking out Air Force command. That RaptorNet has been hijacked will then become obvious to everyone on DARPANET. We can assume a cyber-hunt will begin."

"One you've assured me will never be successful."

"Yes, ma'am. I've structured the hack through a series of proxy accounts that bounce from Hong Kong to Reykjavik to Dallas and back again. The more IP weight is thrown into the search, the more intricate the maze becomes. Regardless, I've left a trail of breadcrumbs that always leads back to the same computer."

"Which is?"

"The one on the president's desk in the Oval Office." Nodwell smiled nastily. "Once they unlock it, a banner unfurls with an image of Dorothy from *Wizard of Oz* saying, 'There's no place like home.'"

"Amusing. Alright. So the cyber-trace goes nowhere. Meanwhile, we're in the driver's seat with RaptorNet."

"Yes." Nodwell drew a laser pen from his pocket and activated it, placing a red dot on the mushroom cloud over Washington, DC. "So per your targeting package, ma'am, Washington, DC is the first city eliminated. Followed by Moscow, Beijing, London and Paris. That will knock out the command-and-control centers of the major nuclear powers. Then we—"

"Talk to me about targeting override."

Nodwell inhaled, changing the direction of his remarks. "If, once we're in, we decide to dispense with your targeting package and go target by target, we introduce a second algorithm that gives us direct fire control. We can hit any target you identify at will."

"What if they bring down the triad?" Her question was sharp. To-the-point. "What if they somehow manage to deactivate the entire land- and sea-based deterrent?"

"It's a possibility," Nodwell admitted. "They've been experimenting with fail-safe tech ever since the early days of the Cold War. I know the system well, but only from a scientific point-of-view. No telling what the Pentagon generals may have up their sleeve. But say they *were* able to throw a switch and power down the triad, we still have options."

"Which are?"

Nodwell clicked off his laser pen, sat and hit a few more buttons on his keyboard. Onscreen, the red mushroom clouds faded to be replaced by a half-dozen gold stars which floated above the Earth in high orbits.

"Our main option is Vanguard." Out came the laser pen again, its red dot traveling from star to star. "Expressly forbidden by international treaty. Its existence unknown to any save the highest level of power in the command-and-control hierarchy. It's the reason we've been aggressively blinding Chinese and Russian satellites for the past two decades. Vanguard represents the ultimate high-ground: a series of orbiting launch platforms capable of delivering warheads from on-high with unparalleled precision. No ICBMs needed. The MIRVs themselves are basically just 'dropped' from the platform onto their designated targets."

"And no way to throw a switch to turn them off."

"Only via RaptorNet. Which we control."

"Which *I* control."

"Er, of course. Ma'am."

Thelma Justice pondered the slowly moving stars for a long moment. "I am thinking perhaps we should start with the orbital platforms," she mused. "It's the last place they're going to expect to see hijacked. If our first nuke comes from there and hits…"

"DC?"

"No." She smiled nastily. "Let's wait and see which cities the White Wolf hits first with the plague. We can adapt our targeting to the evolving crisis."

"Yes, ma'am."

"Improvise. Like jazz musicians." She uttered a laugh. "Make the Americans think the Chinese are doing it. And then once they're convinced of that, we take action suggesting it's the Russians. Or North Koreans. We keep the commanders flummoxed and off-balance while we work our will." She closed her eyes. "*My* will. And when we're done, we destroy this place, evac and move on."

"Yes, ma'am." Nodwell suppressed his feelings of dread and kept working.

CHAPTER THIRTY-EIGHT

AISHA THOUGHT for sure that she would be punished by Thelma Justice for her outburst. Calling the leader of the Order of World Harmony a psychopath while her prisoner was not the behavior of an ally, not was it an ideal survival strategy. Aisha was sure she would be deprived in some way, perhaps even subjected to physical violence. But what Thelma ended up doing to her was worse.

Aisha was removed from the secure rooms she shared with Cody and Sara and relocated to an apartment on another floor. Her first clue that something had changed came when she noted the windows opened onto level ground and were not barred. Then she noticed the absence of mikes and cameras. In the suite she'd shared with Cody and Sara, every room had a prominent surveillance camera. Cody had explained this was a feature of SGI or "small group isolation", a form of incarceration that acted to break down the physical and psychological health of its victims. SGI was recognized internationally as a form of torture. But, for some reason, Aisha was no longer subject to it.

The fullness of Thelma's plan became obvious when she tried the door.

Unlocked.

To her surprise, the door to her suite gave out onto an empty hallway. No armed Fury stood guard. And there were no apparent restrictions on her access to either the stairs or elevator.

I'm free to come and go as I please?

She put it to the test. First, she walked the length of the corridor outside her room. No alarm bells rang, no Furies suddenly appeared to escort her back. So, she tried the elevator, then the stairs. Same result. Her heart clutched in her chest when she tried walking the other corridors. Would she be stopped?

But no. The personnel she encountered – OWH office workers and Furies – passed her with barely a glance. Those who did notice her did so with a flicker of annoyance, indifference. And that's when she understood that she had been 'released' from confinement and monitoring as a show of contempt.

I'm not dangerous enough – or significant enough – to merit attention, she thought. Thelma Justice was as clever as she was cruel. This sort of treatment resonated with Aisha's background as a Muslim woman. For although royalty, she was subject to all the cultural prohibitions of traditional Islam. Her place was *below* her father and *behind* her brothers in preparation for serving *beneath* her future husband. In this, she was something of a nonentity. But here...?

Here I am a minor annoyance, she realized. That was the message Thelma Justice was transmitting to Aisha. It was a clever psychological move – one guaranteed to demoralize. And it stung.

But only for a little while.

———

LIKE GUARDS EVERYWHERE, the Furies followed a routine.

Aisha knew the uniformed women were accustomed to difficult, high-profile assignments. As the visible face of Thelma Justice's organization, they emphasized presence and swagger. They *represented* their boss and took evident pride in that. It was one of the perks of the job.

But more mundane tasks were occasionally required: driving, admin work, monitoring security cameras and crappy details like guarding a locked door. Aisha could monitor the changing of the guard from her window. Within a day, she recognized the faces of the individual guards themselves. These were not Thelma's best.

Makes sense, Aisha thought. *You don't send a thoroughbred to pull a plough.*

Based on the conduct and facial expressions of these guards, she had to wonder if the detail guarding Cody and Sara wasn't some sort of punishment. There was one guard in particular – a smallish woman with a dark complexion. She usually came in the late morning. Despite her tough facial expression, Aisha noted a certain weakness in posture, a wateriness in the eyes.

She's weak, thought Aisha, and zeroed in on her.

Smaller, somewhat clumsy and unburdened by excess intelligence, the Little Guard (as she came to think of her) was obviously the runt of the Furies' litter. Aisha noted how interactions between her and the other uniformed women often seemed to occur at the Little

Guard's expense. Jibes, jokes and insults appeared to flow her way, if what Aisha was seeing through her window was any indication. The Little Guard often walked away from encounters with her co-workers with a clenched jaw and stooped posture, the wateriness in her eyes deepening.

The afternoon Aisha decided to strike, she watched as the Little Guard approached their building at shift change. One of the other Furies crossed her path and evidently saw something she didn't like. Aisha squinted. *An untucked uniform shirt.* The second Fury dressed down the Little Guard in no uncertain terms and then sent her on her way, jaw firm, head down, shoulders hunched.

Aisha retreated to the stairwell, making for the secure housing floor. She arrived and pulled open the fire door, pressing her eyes to the narrow opening, watching as the Little Guard approached and made contact with her co-worker to receive the radio and keys. An exchange occurred which left the Little Guard fuming and the guard she had just relieved laughing. When the Little Guard was alone in the hallway again, she turned, stared at the wall and put her face in her hands.

Aisha slipped into the hallway, a fork from her unit's kitchen in her hands. She crossed the carpeted distance silently in bare feet, approaching the Little Guard from behind...

She lashed out with the fork, aiming for the throat. Expecting a struggle, she was surprised when the tines connected with and plunged into the Little Guard's neck, opening a vein and simultaneously cutting off oxygen. It was a lucky strike. The Little Guard stiffened, trembled briefly and then fell to the carpet, eyes bugged out, mouth opening and closing on nothing as she spasmed.

Aisha lifted the keys from the guard's belt and approached the door. Unlocking it, she saw Cody and Sara sitting talking in the living area. They looked up in surprise when she appeared.

"Come on," she said. "We've got work to do."

CHAPTER THIRTY-NINE

In Athens, Ibrahim Fata finished his prayers. He lingered for a moment, kneeling at the edge of his makeshift prayer rug and bathing in the sweet sense of peace he experienced whenever he finished his devotions. The words of the *sura* rang in his mind...

In the name of Allah, the compassionate and the merciful...

He rose, folded the towel and returned it to the bathroom. Then he washed carefully – face, hands, neck. He even splashed a little water on his hair and combed it with his fingers to straighten it. He was about to execute a martyrdom operation. When it was over, he would leave this world and enter Paradise. It was important to be presentable.

As instructed, he had kept back the steak knife from last night's dinner tray. He located and cleaned it, rinsing the blade in the bathroom sink and drying it with toilet paper. He set it beside the Styrofoam cube on the counter by the sink. He would need the knife to cut the heavy tape binding the stopper of the vial inside.

Ibrahim Fata had almost no education and knew little about science. But he understood that some of his brothers in Crimson Jihad had been conducting experiments, plumbing the wonders of science to create new weapons to bring the fight to the Infidel. He understood that terrible explosions, plague and disease could be stored within small containers, ready to be unleashed when needed. He decided an explosion could not be contained within glass. Therefore, he was likely to be releasing some kind of plague.

Allah…compassionate and merciful …

He knew the disease would kill indiscriminately. Women and children would fall sick. Elders and people of faith – perhaps even some Muslims. He reminded himself not to think about this. Allah was compassionate and merciful. Surely, he would ease the way into Paradise for the innocent, consign the guilty to eternal torment. He himself would die. It was written.

He looked around his room for the last time. Then he put on his shoes and jacket, slipped the knife and Styrofoam cube in his pockets and left.

———

To avoid chance encounters, he took the stairs. They ended at the fire door to the lobby. Holding his breath, he pushed it open. Thankfully, no alarm went off. He was able to slip into the lobby, which was surprisingly busy for an early morning. A glance outside told him that a tour bus had arrived. The group gathering near the registration desk were all members of the same tour group.

Fixing his eyes on the entrance, he bent his steps to the street. Then stopped.

There were two Athens policemen at the desk, engaging earnestly with the manager. While one lifted his radio and spoke into it, the other leaned over a selection of registration cards the manager had laid out on the counter for him to study. As Fata watched, the cop selected three cards and showed them to the manager, who turned and touched three mail slots on the wall behind him, identifying three rooms.

The police were checking the hotel for some reason. And, hardened by jihad in the desert, Ibrahim Fata was not one to make excuses. The police were on the alert, and likely searching for him.

He stepped out onto the sidewalk and began following the route the map he had studied and memorized before burning with a book of hotel matches and flushing the ashes down the toilet. He knew the route was relatively short – had already rehearsed traversing it in his mind a dozen times – and so was surprised when he found himself blocked. Two more policemen stood at the street corner, machine guns slung over their shoulders, giving hard stares to passersby. Occasionally, they would stop one and ask for identification. Something was going on.

He turned into a café and took a seat at a table, picked up a menu and pretended to study it.

There was some sort of city-wide alert underway. Ibrahim Fata could feel the influence of the enemy coiling toward him like tendrils of smoke from some evil fire. He imagined it exuding an odor like brimstone. He had to remain hidden.

A waitress appeared and chattered at him in Greek. Fata smiled, opened the menu and pointed to an item. She nodded, wrote it down on her pad and said something else. At a loss, he merely shook his head. This seemed to satisfy her, and she marched off, notepad in hand to get his order. He waited five minutes, rose and left the restaurant.

The police were still at the intersection. But he saw the mouth of an alley across the street and made for that, careful to keep his steps unhurried. He reached the opposite sidewalk and then disappeared between the buildings, making for the street at the far end. Emerging, he saw no police and so made for the intersection a block down from the pair checking ID. By his reckoning, he could walk up a block and then bypass them one street up before crossing back and continuing the route on the map. He would be late but safe.

He made his way up the street quickly. He saw no more police on the sidewalks, although there was one car parked near his route. When he passed, he saw the young cop inside bent over some paperwork on a clipboard. He continued on his way, his mind filled with images of the map, the cut fence he would find and the road he would follow to the pond where he would dump the vial. He was so engrossed, he failed to register when the police car pulled out of its spot and began following him at a discreet distance.

CHAPTER FORTY

WHEN THE PRESIDENT entered the Oval Office at 1 AM Washington time, the director of CIA was waiting.

"We're all set for you, Mr. President," the director's tone was forthright but uneasy. "Per your instructions, we've utilized our most secure communications satellites and our latest encryption set."

"Excellent." President Harwood, sipping a cup of coffee, took a seat at the Resolute desk and faced the flatscreen monitor that had been wheeled in and placed before it.

"Sir…"

"What is it? Speak frankly."

"Sir, I have to advise against this," the director spoke as one releasing a load of long-held tension. "These men are not official representatives of either their governments or intelligence services. Some of them have been out to pasture for a long, *long* time, sir. My God, Ishigawa hasn't been operational since the Clinton years…"

"Understood." The president held up a hand. "I appreciate your frankness. And your dedication. But we're up to our necks in it with Thelma Justice and now this biowarfare attack. These men have provided solid intelligence and operational support to Cody and Sara Durell throughout. In my opinion, they can be trusted. In fact, right now, they are the *only* people we can trust."

"Yes, sir. Thank you, Mr. President." The director turned to go.

"One more thing."

"Sir?"

The president set down his coffee mug with a click. "I want this kept from Jared Parnell. In fact, I want him isolated. Put him in a goddam padded room if you have to. But I want as much daylight between him and this situation as is possible."

"Yes, sir. I'll see to it right away."

"Excellent." Harwood hit the transmit button on his intercom. "Okay, I'm ready. Pipe them in."

As the director let himself out of the room, closing the door behind him, the screen before the president gleamed to life. The secure videoconference link simultaneously joined him and the other members of the meeting, who were scattered across several time zones, each visible in a separate square. In the top left was Horace Parsons, retired MI-6 and the nominal head of the Backchannel network, ensconced in his office in Moscow. In the square beside his, Hamid Hassan was visible transmitting from a secure location in Syria. Below Parsons was Ishigawa in Amman. The square beside him and below Hamid was dark, with a single red light pulsing in its lower right corner.

"Gentlemen," said the president. "I want to start by saying what an honor it is to meet you. Until now, the existence of the ad-hoc Backchannel network was only a rumor. But I'm pleased to say that rumor has been confirmed a reality by the astute and valorous support you have shown my operatives in the field. Gentlemen, America owes you all a great debt."

Each man reacted characteristically. Parsons offered a nod of thanks. Hamid smiled and shrugged. Ishigawa offered a deep and serious bow.

"Because of your work, our defense staff has been alerted to the effort to spread smallpox internationally by members of Crimson Jihad." Harwood sipped his coffee. "I have instructed CIA to work with Joint Special Operations Command in the Pentagon to coordinate a response. I'm asking that you gentlemen assist us by forwarding any additional information you may have."

At this point, Parsons spoke up. "Horace Parsons here, sir, late of Her Majesty's Secret Service. We've pulled together a report for you, sir. It contains everything my colleague Mr. Ishigawa and his hacker friends have been able to discover about the courier flights and present disposition of Crimson Jihad agents in the west. I believe we also have some additional data on Jack Cody and Sara Durell."

Harwood sat forward. "Where are they?"

Hamid Hassan spoke up. "Hello from Syria, Mr. President. We sent Jack Cody across the border into Jordan. Mr. Ishigawa was able to get him into Italy. Our best info now is that he is in the north of the country, in the Italian Alps."

"Thelma Justice has mountain villa there," said Ishigawa. "We have, ah, rumors of Vetrov's arrival. Cody, Sara Durell and Princess Aisha are believed to be prisoners there."

"Okay, then." Harwood nodded and sat back. "Chances are that's where the operation is being coordinated from. Gentlemen, thank you."

"I will send that report to you now, Mr. President," promised Parsons. "Should be with you shortly."

"Excellent. On behalf of a grateful nation, my thanks."

The Backchannel operatives responded with nods and smiles. The president closed the call. The three filled squares darkened. The blinking red light in the fourth turned green and went live.

President Harwood stared into the face of Achmed bint-Ahmed, the newly-crowned Emirati sheikh. The old sheikh had been a valued colleague in international affairs. His death left a huge vacuum in the Middle East.

"Your Majesty," said the president. "Thank you for making time to speak to me."

"Not at all, Mr. President." Sheikh Achmed gave a tired smile. Gone was the anxious and impulsive heir ready to burn the world in his nation's interest. Now sheikh, Achmed had relaxed into the seat of power with a calm magnanimity worthy of the noblest royals. "Our father valued his relationship with you and your country enormously. That is a tradition that will continue under my reign, sir. The Emirates are both your ally and at your service. How can I help you today?"

"Actually, I think it is *I* who can help you, Your Majesty." Harwood smiled. "I have recently been in contact with agents who are working a problem of international scope. We face a terrible crisis. In gathering together intelligence, we have come across information that may be of interest to you. Sir, I believe we have discovered the location of your sister, the princess."

At this, Sheikh Achmed leaned toward the camera.

"Mr. President," he said slowly. "Please tell me *everything* you know."

CHAPTER FORTY-ONE

THE WHITE WOLF returned to Thelma Justice's chateau; his heart burdened with worry.

He was accustomed to running his own operations on his own terms. This concept of sharing a burden with Infidels like Vetrov and Justice never sat comfortably with him. (And the notion of a *woman* exercising any sort of military leadership was ludicrous in the extreme!) But he had long ago learned to master his impatience, to temper his expectations. Compromises, he realized, would be necessary on the road of jihad.

What matters in the end is a victory for Allah and the Q'uran, he reminded himself, as he had so many times before.

A light snow was falling as the helicopter lowered itself metre by shuddery metre toward the large patio that served as a landing site. It touched down, the rotors touching off a blizzard of snow. As they slowed, the snow settled and the bald, black woman in overalls whom he recognized from previous visits approached.

"Thelma Justice has asked me to conduct you to the

control room, sir." The woman's tone was neutral, but he sensed the tension in her voice. *I have been the topic of some conversation,* he thought. And from the sound of things, it hadn't been a pleasant discussion.

They entered through the steel doorway and took a staircase down to the office level. The woman in overalls conducted him to the doorway of the room full of cubicles over which Thelma Justice presided. She was awaiting him.

"I am glad you have decided to return." She rose as he stalked down the row between the cubicles where Nodwell and three other lab techs sat, heads down over their screens. "We're approaching a point of fruition... Or, rather, *should* be. What have you found out about your operative in Rome?"

"There was a man who came to his hotel." The White Wolf stopped before her desk and crossed his arms. "This man – or, *men* because it's hard to say whether it's one man who changed his appearance or several – attacked and subdued my jihadi. From all appearances, he threw this brother out the window."

Thelma slapped her desk in frustration.

"If they have found this brother, it is reasonable to surmise that the hunt is now on for others," he said. "We should prepare to move with all speed."

He paused and looked around.

"Where is General Vetrov?" he asked. And Thelma Justice smiled.

"She shot him," Nodwell's voice was soft but clear in the sterile silence of the control room. "Blew his brains out. It was inevitable, really. If you understand anything about evolution."

"Where are we with launch staging?" she asked him sharply.

"Oh, systems are nominal," replied Nodwell. To the White Wolf, he said, "She's evolved beyond the need for Vetrov. Or men. Or, apparently, human decency and compassion altoge—"

"*Quiet!*" Thelma Justice narrowed her eyes at the scientist. His words were insubordinate, but he understood the precarity of her position with him. She couldn't simply dispose of him as she had with the Russian – not so long as he was needed to bring RaptorNet operational. That bought him a certain latitude. But not much.

"You killed Vetrov?" The White Wolf's voice had softened. There was a hollow quality to these words. He experienced the unfamiliar sensation of fear.

"Welcome to the revolution," she said with a smile.

The old desert warrior struggled to control himself. He understood that, out in the world, he was as much in danger as anyone else once the virus was released. The plan was to remain here, to see it through with Thelma and Vetrov. Now the knowledge that he was alone with this powerful woman, surrounded by her loyal force of Amazons gave him pause.

Vetrov was dead.

The world was about to be reduced to a biological wasteland.

And he was completely alone.

"When do you intend to strike?" he asked coldly.

"Within the hour." Thelma's eyed slid to the clock. "My man Nodwell here tells me the best way to gain control of RaptorNet is to sneak up on it. Apparently, there is a shift change that occurs at the National Military Command Center right around this time. That's the window we need to throw out a grappling hook and tug this thing in. We grab it, take control and start firing before anyone notices or mounts a resistance. The whole thing will be over in minutes."

"My men are ready to begin delivering the virus. The first one has already been activated. Others will follow shortly."

"You're running one to see how it goes and iron out all the bugs." Her voice held real approval. "That's a good plan, my friend. If we time this right, emergency rooms should start filling up just as the first bombs begin to fall."

The White Wolf shook his head in wonder. A biowarfare attack followed by a spectrum-wide nuclear strike. It was a plan as ruthless and insidious as any he had ever conceived. It was Infinite Justice. It was Endgame.

What a madwoman, he thought. And wondered how Allah planned to turn this nightmare to His purpose.

"What then?" he asked.

"We wait for the worst of the radiation to clear." Thelma Justice turned to face the big screen and crossed her arms. "For the worst of the disease to have passed. Months? Perhaps a year? Then we enter the splendid cities! My women! Dressed in their biohazard suits, bearing food and medicine and the divine truth that *we* – women! – are now to seize and hold the stage. We who should guide humanity forward…"

The White Wolf stood impassively as she spoke. But with each passing word it became ever clearer that the post-nuclear landscape would be every bit the battlefield of the modern world. He and his followers could not live under such a regime. There would be war. But some time in the future. For now, he had to bide his time.

One war at a time, he thought. And smiled.

CHAPTER FORTY-TWO

"THERE MUST BE an armory somewhere in this place."
Cody edged cautiously down the hallway, his words a
clear whisper in the building's stillness. Sara was directly
behind him. And behind her, last in the column, crept
Aisha, who kept an eye on the corridor behind them.

"I believe it's here, on three," Aisha said. "The guards
usually check in at that room at the end of the hallway."
She pointed toward an unmarked oak door. A card-
reader adorned the wall beside it. Cody guessed it func-
tioned as the team room. It made sense they would store
radios and weapons there. Cody drew them down an
alcove that led to the washrooms about twenty yards up
from the door.

"Aisha, I want you to go knock," he said. "Tell them
there's trouble in the lobby and a guard has been injured.
Give it an Academy Award performance. Got it?"

Aisha nodded. As Cody watched she took several
fast, deep breaths, shook her head to muss her hair and
then sprinted to the door. She pounded on it in a fevered
panic. A longish silence followed. When she began

punching it again, she managed two blows before the door was jerked open. A uniformed Fury leaned out, body quivering with anger.

"What are—?"

"Please come quickly!" Aisha stamped her foot for emphasis. "There's been an incident in the lobby! A guard is injured." The Fury started and then stepped out of the room, pulling the door shut behind her. She followed Aisha at a trot and made it as far as the alcove before Cody clotheslined her. Perfect impact: the bone of his forearm smacked her dead center on the top lip between nose and mouth, hard enough to stun her. The drop to the floor put her out.

"Get her badge," he told Sara as he relieved the unconscious Fury of her gun belt. As Sara pulled the lanyard loose and used the ID card there to open the door, Cody grabbed the prone woman by her shoulders and dragged her through the doorway. As Cody had suspected, inside was a team room. Radios lined the top of a filing cabinet. A computer sat on the desktop, a rack of machine-guns on the wall behind it. Cody stepped over to examine the weapons.

Vetrov must be supplying them with their small-arms, Cody thought. The racks held ten PP-2000 machine-pistols. Unveiled to the world in 2004, they were relative newcomers to the Russian security arsenal. But they had already proven their worth by being selected as one of the two standard SMGs of the Russian police services. A compact 13.5 inches when the stock was folded, the PP-2000 weighed a mere three pounds fully loaded. The weapon was capable of firing 600 rounds of 9x19mm Parabellum rounds per minute and came with an extra 40 round detachable box magazine doing double-duty as a fixed stock. He pulled one down and handed it to Sara.

"Well, here's a nice little surprise," she said, snapping the bolt and checking the chamber. "Looks like I'm well stocked. About 80 rounds."

"I'm about the same." Cody checked over his own weapon. "We need to get to the control room where they've hijacked RaptorNet."

"We going to force them to cede control?"

"No time. We'll just blow the place. That ought to scrub whatever plans they've cooked up. Aisha, you stay behind me, got it? Mirror my movements. If I start running, keep up with me. If I drop, hit the deck. Understand?"

"I understand." She nodded. She did not ask for a gun but noted a collapsible ASP baton holstered on a utility belt hanging from the gun rack. She groped for the baton's handle and drew it out. The black, six-inch tube was surprisingly heavy. She depressed the blue release button and flicked her wrist. Sixteen inches of black titanium shaft leapt into the air. The shaft ended in a heavy, flat steel disc. Its edges were beveled and almost sharp. Aisha knew from experience how much damage an ASP baton could inflict. She had once seen her father's bodyguard use one against a trespasser in the palace. One casual flick of the weapon had snapped the man's kneecap. Aisha resolved to aim for skulls.

"We go in hard," Cody was saying to Sara. "Through the doorway simultaneously. You take the right side of the room. I'll take the left. We kill anything that moves."

"Works for me." Sara racked the machine-pistol. "Let's do this."

"Okay." Cody went to the door, softly turned the knob and opened it just a crack. Voices could be heard in the corridor outside. He closed the door carefully, then turned. "Damn," he whispered.

"How many?" Sara whispered.

Cody held up four fingers.

Sara turned back to the gun rack. With a small noise of surprise, she held up her Beretta and Cody's.

"We've got our sidearms back. And my silencer is still here." She put down her machine-pistol and picked up her Beretta with her right hand. Her left hand dipped into a sheath on the holster and emerged holding a matte black suppressor. She screwed it into the end of the Beretta's barrel, eyes on the door, working by feel.

Cody, meanwhile, nodded and took up a position behind the door with both hands on the knob. Aisha could tell from the way he positioned his legs and feet that his plan was to pull and spring, yanking the door wide and giving Sara an uninterrupted field of fire. Aisha moved behind the steel filing cabinet holding the radios and crouched, the ASP baton held point downward, parallel with her leg.

Sara breathed deeply, calming herself. Then she turned to Cody and nodded, holding up a hand with three fingers raised. *Three.* She dropped a finger. *Two...one...*

Cody yanked wide the door.

Sara's arm swept up, the silenced Beretta centered on the first of four Furies. She knew she could dispatch them all within 4.8 seconds, her record at the Agency's range in Quantico. And she was planning to do just that. When her gun jammed.

CHAPTER FORTY-THREE

"THAT'S IT." Nodwell sat back from his computer and stretched. "We've snuck in and sealed all the back doors behind us. RaptorNet has been functionally ours for an hour. Now it's completely ours. Everyone else is sealed out. All the targeting telemetry has been loaded and installed per your instructions. We've firewalled off the entire switching hub for that sector of Pentagon space command. Not only do we own the castle, but we own the neighborhood and the land a hundred miles in every direction. Congratulations, Ms. Justice…"

At her desk, Thelma Justice rose, her heart beating furiously in her chest.

"You now own the largest, most sophisticated nuclear weapons command and control system ever devised."

She did. She *did,* dammit. Thelma took a moment to savor her victory. That, too, was entirely hers. Aside from the White Wolf, there was nobody left with whom to share the laurels. Vetrov was dead. Tiff Butler was dead.

Only she, Thelma Justice, had won through. Last woman standing. Empress.

Queen.

The White Wolf entered the room. She turned to him. "Where is the first bio-weapon attack due to occur again?" she asked.

He turned and measured the flatscreen image with his steady gaze. "Here." He marched forward until he was directly below the screen. "The eastern portion of the Mediterranean. That was where the first flights landed. Athens. Here…"

Thelma Justice toggled the controls. A gold square hovered over the Peloponnesus. Crete and the Dardanelles were also visible. With a punch of the button, the Greek mainland appeared, Athens highlighted as a winking red dot.

"Nodwell. How's our targeting in that region?"

"Easily within reach of our sub-based platforms. Also within reach from orbital platforms. I have a full yield capacity on that region."

She considered. "Hold off on Athens. For now. Let's wait until the hospitals and emergency rooms are packed, then do a medium-sized airburst over the country. Let radiation sickness pile onto the plague numbers and we'll have real misery there. No. Strike someplace first that would likely be used as a staging area for assistance. Say..?"

"Rome?" suggested Nodwell.

"Sure." She nodded. "Say Rome and Istanbul both. Start with Istanbul. That will be target one. Followed by…"

Rome.

The word hovered in the air, unsaid. Everyone, including the White Wolf, waited to hear her say it. But she drifted off because of something she thought she might have heard. A sharp sound like a...

Gunshot?

No. The alarms would be going off in the chateau.

"Rome," she said finally. "Then we need to think about using the weapons strategically to trigger war between competing powers ..."

———

SARA's GUN JAMMED. And three things happened in quick succession.

The first was that the two guards with their backs to her turned, seeing her for the first time and grasping at their sidearms.

The second was that Aisha stepped forward and slammed the ASP baton into the skull of the first and then second of these two guards. Their skullcaps split with an audible *crack!* and they both sank like deflated balloons.

The third was that one of the remaining two guards had successfully drawn her sidearm and was about to fire it when Cody stepped forward, grasped her arm and pushed it skyward. The pistol went off – a single shot – before Cody knocked her unconscious with a hammer-blow to the neck.

The last guard spun and aimed for the stairs. She made it three steps before Sara was on her, tackling her down, neutralizing her with a rear naked choke. Within twenty seconds, the guard was spasming into unconsciousness. Sara rolled from the woman's snoring form and stood.

"I'm gonna start calling you slugger." Sara grinned

and chucked Aisha on the shoulder. "That's four down. How many more do you figure Thelma has left?"

"She has a force of two hundred who guard the chateau."

"Okay, then. Four down. One hundred ninety-six to go."

"That's the spirit," said Cody. "Now let's dispose of these four."

Using the first guard's magnetic ID card, they accessed the team room and dragged the prone forms inside. Then they re-mustered in the corridor, checked their weapons and waited to see if the shot generated a response. It did not.

"So we're far enough into a remote section that it wasn't noticed." Sara hoisted her machine-pistol into place. "There's an extra tactical advantage. And I can think of another one."

Her eyes went back to the door of the team room.

"What are you thinking?" Cody asked.

Sara inclined her head. *Let's go back in just for a sec.* Cody shrugged and acquiesced. He watched as Sara entered the room and knelt beside one of the unconscious Furies. Checking the cuffs and collar of the woman's uniform, she thought for a moment before turning to Cody.

"This one would fit me. That one?" She nodded to another prone Fury. "With a little adjusting could fit Aisha."

Cody grinned. "And me?"

"You're the prize." Sara stood and examined a rack of handcuffs and restraints by the rifles. "I believe we have something in your size... Here."

Sara reached out and grasped something dark within the folds of hand- and ankle-cuff paraphernalia. Cody caught it one-handed and held it up. It was a bag of closely-stitched black nylon mesh with a draw-string tie around its mouth. From his time visiting correctional facilities in the course of his duties, he recognized the item for what it was.

"You want me to wear a spit mask?"

"Think of it as the male equivalent of a burqa."

Aisha, to both of their surprise, giggled.

And so five minutes later, each wearing a Fury uniform, beret and hair arranged to disguise their faces, Sara and Aisha emerged from the team room, pushing Cody between them, his face and head covered by a spit mask.

CHAPTER FORTY-FOUR

In Athens, Ibrahim Fata bypassed the police checkpoint by one block, then returned to the original route laid out by the map. He stepped back onto the street a block behind the two policemen checking papers. Then, casting a final glance over his shoulder at them, he proceeded down the street toward the area with the fence which had been pre-cut to allow his passage. Two blocks further on, he found it.

You will find the fence cut in a triangular pattern. You will go through.

Sure enough, the frost fence had been sliced in a discreet diagonal by a set of wire-cutters. He knelt and drew up the triangular section of fence. So engrossed was he in this that he did not register the police car braking to a halt a half-block away.

Ibrahim Fata wiggled under the fence, stood and bent the grid back into place, doing his best to make it look undisturbed. He turned. The fence was at the top of a slight rise. Below and off to his left was a concrete ribbon of road. He cast his mind back to the call...

You will follow the hill to the paved road, and the paved road down to the aquifer.

It resembles a small pond, he remembered. He was to gain the aquifer, produce the Styrofoam cube, remove the vial and cut it open using the steak knife in his right coat pocket. Then he was to dump the contents of the vial into the water before smashing the glass container and brushing all its pieces into the water, as well.

Soon after, I will die, he thought. And praised Allah.

He was halfway down the hill to the road when he heard the voice raised behind him:

"Oi!"

He stopped and turned.

A uniformed policeman was hustling down the slope toward him. Fata remained calm, slipping one hand into his right coat pocket and another into his breast pocket. The cop had not drawn his weapon and did not appear to be in any particular hurry. But Fata could tell from the guy's posture and attitude that he was definitely making a stop – stepping in because he was trespassing in a restricted area. So Fata did what was likeliest the most predictable thing in the cop's experience: he produced ID and began blathering in his local dialect.

Seeing this, the policeman slowed, held up a hand and smiled. When he spoke, his words were Greek and delivered in a tone of reassurance. He took the laminated ID card Fata handed him, glanced down at the photo and back up to compare it to the face. He asked a question.

Fata smiled, shrugged and shook his head.

The cop sighed and shook his head. He turned the ID card over, read the back and then reached up to hit the transmit button on his radio mic. He spoke briefly, then awaited a response.

Fata swallowed, shifting from foot to foot. The cop was in contact with someone now. He planned to wait until the cop was done on the radio before making a move. Meanwhile, the conversation the cop was having with dispatch continued.

Fata began to think that perhaps he wouldn't have to kill this policeman. That perhaps his provision of fake identity and a proforma radio check would be sufficient. That perhaps he could send this man who seemed, from outward appearance, to be a decent enough fellow. Possibly a family man. Fata noted little things about the cop, like how he kept an eye on him as he spoke, but also a smile so as not to seem intimidating. He noticed the man wore some sort of religious medallion under his shirt. And the finger for wedding rings, the one on the left hand, held a band of gold.

He's a patient man, Fata thought. *Probably a father.*

Fata thought he might have made it. Until something spoken on the other end of the radio caused the policeman's eyebrow to twitch and the edge of his smirk to turn downward. The eye contact, when it came this time, was not friendly.

Something was wrong.

Now the cop was nodding, his hand dropping to his handcuff case. With a final word he signed off, then opened and unholstered his nearest set of cuffs. He held out one hand, forefinger extended, and twirled it in the air. *Turn around.* Fata smiled in recognition, smiled broadly and nodded. He made as if to turn...

His right hand flashed out of his pocket, the steak knife driving, point-forward, into the cop's stomach. It hit and ripped through the layers of uniform and skin with surprising ease. The policeman had been about to say something starting with the sound of 'ch' but the syllable froze on his lips.

"*Ch…ch…h…h…*"

Fata gripped and regripped the knife handle more firmly, then twisted it hard sideways. The cop, if he had anything else to say, found it impossible. His breath was all hitched up around the pain and surprise in his gut. Fata pushed down on the handle, then drove the knife upwards. The policeman's eyes crossed, breath hissed from his throat, and he teetered forward, done. Collapsing on the grass, he twitched once and then lay still.

His radio crackled, and a voice came from the other end, insistent and worried.

A long pause, a wave of crackling. Then silence. The policeman lay very, very still. Fata turned and studied the way back. Fresh footprints in the grass and the cut section of fence twisted upward. Plus, the police car parked nearby. Odd, but they were in a quiet section of the city. He would remain undiscovered for a while.

He turned and examined the way forward.

Somewhere along the paved road below, a large pond of drinking water supplied the daily needs of the city of Athens. By dropping the contents of the test tube in there, Ibrahim Fata would be condemning three million people to death.

Without another thought, he began descending the hill toward the road.

CHAPTER FORTY-FIVE

THE THREE OF them strode along the middle of the hallway, the two women behind Cody, heads down, machine-pistols cradled in their arms while he stumbled up ahead, blinded by the spit bag's black mesh, wrists loosely cuffed in front – so loosely, in fact, that a sudden movement would jar the steel circlets from his wrists. Cody had to take care to keep his knuckles turned upward to avoid the cuffs falling off.

The rooms around them seemed to be filling up. During lulls in hallway activity, Sara narrated what she saw. "Looks like we've got Furies gathering," she muttered. "I've counted about seventy-five in the past few minutes. Some are wearing parkas and outerwear, looking like maybe they've just tumbled off of busses."

"She's gathering her staff," Aisha noted.

Beneath the mesh, Cody frowned. The odds on their control room strike were growing longer by the minute. Three against eight or ten were one thing. But against seventy-five...?

"More ahead," Sara whispered. And shoved him. "Quit foot-dragging," she snapped, loud enough to draw approving glances from the passing Furies.

Now they were descending the stone and steel staircase to the control room. Cody heard Sara and then Aisha snap the safeties off their machine-pistols. Things were going to start happening very soon.

As they reached the first landing and turned toward the next set of stairs, Aisha's hands came up and unfastened the neck of the spit-hood. Once Cody's hands were free, he could remove it easily. He flexed his fists, breathing deeply, psyching himself into the zone.

A voice came over the PA system:

"Alert One... Security breach... Three escapees..."

Instantly, all eyes were on Cody, Sara and Aisha.

"GET THEM!"

And the chatter of semi-automatic weapons fire echoed in the stairwell. Cody dropped the cuffs from his wrists, pushed up the spit mask and grappled the Beretta from its place in the small of his back. Behind him and slightly to his right, Sara was already engaged, returning fire from two Furies at the door to the control room.

"Looks like our plan went sideways!" he cried.

"Every plan is perfect until it meets the enemy!" She paused to fire off a burst. "Well, here we are!"

A blast of weapons fire from the stairs above them: Aisha was there, having grabbed up a weapon from a fallen Fury, she was joining the fight. Together, the three of them coordinated fire as they advanced down the stairwell, taking advantage of the high ground. One of the Furies in the doorway fell. Cody snapped off two rounds at the second one, driving her back inside for cover.

"Come on!" He rushed downstairs two at a time toward the control room door. Sara was right behind him, PP-2000 raised and ready. Aisha was doing a slow climb down behind them, raking the area with bursts of suppressing fire. The door to the control room lay just ahead.

And now suddenly a dozen appeared, having doubtless entered by some rear entry. They formed a defensive line just outside the door and raised their weapons. Had they been a little sharper, they might have taken down one or more of them. But a few seconds lag in battlefield discipline left Cody, Sara and Aisha ample time to dive back behind a jumbled pile of reception area furniture. It provided the perfect redoubt.

"Where the hell did they all come from?" Sara shook her head as she swapped out magazines.

"That would be Thelma's Scarlet Guard," Aisha said. "Her elite personal bodyguard."

"Elite." Sara rolled her eyes. "Okay."

Cody cleared his throat but said nothing. Megalomaniacs and power-hungry psychopaths always seemed to have a military fetish. He recalled Gaddafi and his all-female bodyguard, and Amin's feared 'suicide squad' militias. The myths that their guys were anything more than rent-a-cops with guns was reinforced by grandiose titles.

He and Sara, on the other hand, were alumni of the American special forces' community.

"Forty-two," he said. "Sixty-eight. Hike!"

"Wide and long?" She grinned. "Or straight in through the front door?"

"Front door," he said. "We don't have much time."

She reached into a slim hip pouch and drew out two narrow cylinders about the width of her palms. A red button sat atop each. At a nod from Cody, she pressed these, aimed and tossed both tubes at the assembled rank of Furies.

The explosions ripped through the lobby like a sudden burst of artillery. A bolt of lightning tore through the room sideways, ripping the ranks of uniformed women in half. The ones not immediately shattered were deafened, blinded, dazed and wandering the scene with their hands clasping their ears until Cody and Sara mowed them down.

The door to the control room was clear. Sections on either side had been blasted away so the effect was now more circular than rectangular. Beyond lay wreckage, smoking furniture and tangled sections of cubicles. As they advanced, a rank of Furies appeared behind the piled sections, locking and loading and preparing to engage.

"Got any more of those handy lipstick grenades?" Cody asked hopefully.

"Just one." She produced it.

"Here. Let's have it." He grasped it as she put it into his hand, then drew them both to cover as the first salvo from inside the control room blasted through the ruined doorway.

"Here." Cody pressed a rangefinder into Sara's hands. "See what you can spot with that. I want to get a sense of what's going on in there."

He smacked home a fresh magazine into his Beretta, rose and scattered the front rank of defenders with a series of well-placed shots. They dove for cover just as Sara rose and scanned the scene beyond the doorway with the rangefinder. After one quick pass right to left and back again, she sank behind the redoubt of torn and buckled furniture.

"Anything?" Cody asked.

"Yes. It looks like they're about to bring RaptorNet live."

"Okay. Aisha…" He turned. And that's when they both realized she was gone.

CHAPTER FORTY-SIX

Two FLOORS DOWN, in another part of the complex, Aisha bint al-Ahmad, Princess of the Emirates and sister of the Sheikh, moved with predatory silence. Moved as if her life depended upon it because it did.

She had caught a glimpse of a man she recognized – a man she remembered from the briefings following the assassination of her Uncle Fahd, brother of her father the Sheikh, by operatives of Crimson Jihad. The Emirates' own intelligence service gave them a thorough briefing, along with agents of the CIA, sent at President Harwood's request. America and the world took the loss seriously.

But none so seriously as the princess.

"What is the answer, O wise and learned one?" Fahd would smile, examining 14-year-old Aisha over the tops of his reading bifocals. "Remember there are always two alternatives."

"There is either a known answer or one that is unknown," she would reply. "And if unknown, we must discover it."

"Because that is how we, whom Allah has gifted with intelligence, may serve the world."

It was Fahd who set her feet on the path to learning, Fahd who had encouraged her to explore even the most obscure avenues of study. He insisted there was nothing in the Q'uran forbidding a woman to exercise her intellectual talents. Fahd had promised that when she became old enough, he would allow her to accompany him on one of his peace envoys.

"... that is how we, whom Allah has gifted with intelligence, may serve the world..."

It was during the briefing following his assassination that she realized: she had actually *seen* one of the terrorists herself – the one called Mustafa who was the White Wolf's right hand. He had managed to sneak aboard Uncle Fahd's jet, disguised as a member of the flight crew. He had stood out to her because of his dark, Nigerian skin and unkempt beard. Later, images of him placing the bomb and then deplaning at a stopover captured via CCTV had confirmed it. She had *seen* the man in person.

She had told no one.

And now she had seen him again.

Crouching on the stairwell with Cody and Sara, she had caught the barest glimpse of the man slipping into an elevator during a lull in the gunfight. She had followed, arriving as the doors slid closed and the light panel above the elevator began winking. Descent: he had journeyed down to a level called B-3. She summoned an elevator and followed.

The chateau was large and sophisticated enough to encompass multiple underground sectors. She paused at B-2 and peeked out of the car. It resembled a vast warehouse, with shelves of high steel rising into the underground shadows. Aisha saw canned foodstuffs, equipment and survival supplies to last years. Then she descended another floor and to explore B-3.

The first thing that hit her was the sound of splashing water. She sensed humidity in the air. She guessed that perhaps there was a cistern or drinking water cache down here. But then she noticed ribbons of light dancing on the ceiling and recognized them as light reflected from water. *Waves,* she thought. A low rumbling sound intruded, coming from up ahead. She followed the corridor, noting the carpeting beneath her feet give way to tile and then concrete.

The lights dimmed in this part of the facility, and two sensations hit her at once: a damp, frigid cold and the sharp stench of gasoline. The cement walls became a patchwork of old brick and mortar. *These tunnels are old,* she realized. In olden times, people had used the underground rivers in the region for transport.

A voice cried out in Italian, and she heard a splash. Coming to the wall's edge, Aisha peered around.

The corridor ended at an underground pier. The pier projected out into a vast underground lake. Within the arch of a high cave ceiling studded with stalactites, an underground tunnel and river system kept the chateau connected to the outside world, despite its remoteness. Now the man named Mustafa stood on the edge of the pier, awaiting an approaching boat. It was a cabin cruiser – a small Sargo of the kind favored by sport fisherman. In this case, it was trim and low enough in the water to be the craft of choice to navigate the labyrinthine, low-ceilinged caves.

Aisha knew without having to check who was likely onboard. It would be the White Wolf himself – the one who had killed her uncle. Reflecting on this, Aisha gripped and regripped her PP-2000.

It was payback time.

The Sargo approached the pier as she slipped out, machine-pistol raised and made for the pier. Mustafa heard her footsteps and turned.

"*Mutu!*" she hissed. As Mustafa fumbled in his robes for a gun, she brought up the PP-2000 and opened fire, allowing her finger to clamp hard on the trigger and directing the spray of bullets directly into the man. Mustafa jerked and twitched like a puppet in the storm of lead, jitterbugging back across the pier until he fell backwards into the drink, his weapon still unfired.

Aisha rushed to the edge of the pier and began peppering the Sargo with rounds. The man at the wheel ducked. The White Wolf did likewise, taking refuge behind the cabin. His body man brought up his own weapon and trained it on Aisha. He managed two shots before she blew him away in a hail of fury and lead.

"*Come out here and face me you COWARD!*" she shrieked at the White Wolf. "*Come out here and meet the doom Allah has brought you in the form of a WOMAN!*"

She fired again, shredding the glass and hull of the Sargo. The blood from White Wolf's body man was slopping over the deck to stain the side. The boat was now moving in a tight circle away from the pier. The bullets she chased it with made waves in the underground lake.

CHAPTER FORTY-SEVEN

THELMA JUSTICE's Furies put up an ample resistance. As the countdown proceeded behind them, they fought rank on rank from behind their rampart of upended office furniture and cubicles. When Cody and Sara regrouped and brought the fight to them again, they found a determined and well-entrenched enemy.

Sara made an attempt to flank them. Cody provided covering fire, but she could find insufficient cover along her route of attack and so was forced to retreat. Then it was Cody's turn. He tried from the opposite side and had no better luck. Although he did get a glimpse of the big control board and brought news back to Sara when he withdrew.

"They're getting set for a big strike," he told her. "The target board is all lit up. But it's clever. She's going for global infrastructure – harbors and airports and the like. She's cutting us off from each other. Then she's likely going to attack again."

"That on top of the plague. Okay." Sara eyed the

explosive tube. "Time to go through the front door one more time."

"Ready when you are." Cody proffered the explosive.

"You're the big football hero." She passed him the explosive. "Show us how it's done, sport."

"Can do. Take cover." Cody turned and sized up the distance between their position and the Furies' defensive line. He squinted, calmed his breath, waited…and then threw. The cylinder arced end over end and lodged itself dead center at the top of the debris pile. An instant later, it detonated. With a concussive *bloom!* the shockwave blew the defensive works apart, scattering bodies hither and yon. Cody and Sara seized up their machine-pistols and charged.

The remaining few Furies were dazed or unconscious. Cody made quick work of the nearest ones while Sara mopped up the rear guard. It took them less than a minute to take and hold the center. The surviving Furies were dropping back to the last row of unoccupied cubicles. A row or two ahead of that, Thelma Justice's team worked on the targeting plan. At the head of the room, Thelma Justice paced on her podium, an eye on the fighting in back.

"Can you get her from here?" Sara squinted into the smoke at the madwoman up front.

"We've still got the home team to deal with!" Cody snatched up a fallen guard's machine-pistol and engaged the next rank of Furies. At the same time, Sara fell to with a vengeance and the slaughter began afresh.

These second stringers weren't the tough gals who had faced them at the front door. These were the lieutenants, the admin officers, the clerks. These were the beta-Furies – the ones that knew how to survive but little else. And because they cared more about their own skin than about winning, Cody and Sara made quick work of them. Within minutes, they were mopping up and securing a position at the last row of cubicles.

Thelma Justice pounded her desk with her fists and roared: *"Get them!"*

A scattering of Furies, perhaps a half-dozen, jogged out to face Cody and Sara. The rest were white-coated scientists and engineers. All but Nodwell had stopped what they were doing and were looking up at each other with a *'who, me?'* look on their faces.

"Yes! You! Pick up a gun and kill them!"

One of the white-coated techs bent and hesitantly picked up a gun from a fallen Fury. Two others tentatively followed suit.

"Good! Yes! Now!" She leveled a finger at Cody and Sara. "Kill them!"

Cody and Sara exchanged a look, racked the actions on their machine-pistols and waded into the rabble.

The half-assed Furies were the first to fall. The most eager to show their devotion, they died first, twisting in place and collapsing. They danced as they were riddled by withering machine-gun fire. They were the easiest to dispose of.

The scientist types proved remarkably tougher. Beginner's luck most likely, was Cody's assessment. They were overly cautious, tentative with their weapons. This made them miss more but caused them to conserve ammunition. They had to be flushed out first. Like rats.

Sara worked up the right side of the corridor between cubicles, blasting anything that moved. Her preemptive fire into a cubicle wall dropped two whitecoats. But a third who had been hiding next cubicle up popped out, firing from her knees. She missed Sara's center mass. But her round creased the outer edge of Sara's boot, close enough to generate a sensation of warmth in her foot. She put the whitecoat down with a double-tap – two shots in quick succession to the chest. The knee-shooter tumbled and spilled onto the carpet.

Cody worked his way methodically up the left side. His style was less cautious than Sara's, so he moved more quickly. But he had lower quality targets. Most of the whitecoats cowered away the moment they saw him, making easy pickings. The odd feisty one either shot wide or couldn't manage the gun and so died under Cody's hail of bullets. This continued until Cody came to one last guy, a chubby, balding man with glasses.

"I guess you'd be the good guys," he muttered, favoring Cody with a glance.

"Hands up," said Cody, levelling the machine-pistol on him.

Nodwell sighed, sat back from the computer and put his hands up. "Talk about the nick of time," he said. "Another thirty seconds and it would have been Armageddon."

Those were his last words. A bullet hole suddenly appeared in his forehead.

Cody turned to see Thelma Justice extending a nickel-plated revolver at the end of her right arm. Her shot had killed Nodwell cleanly. She waved a hand at a flashing red button on the desk before her.

"I press this and the whole chateau goes up," she taunted. Right before reaching out, pushing the button and then fleeing through a rear door.

CHAPTER FORTY-EIGHT

IBRAHIM FATA REACHED the paved road at the base of the hill and began following it, as instructed. He left the body of the dead policeman he had stabbed lying where it had fallen. It would eventually draw attention, but not until he had completed his mission. And after that, he didn't care what happened to him. He would die soon anyway. His martyrdom was scheduled – no longer a possibility but an impending fact.

He found his thoughts drifting back to the village where he had grown up. He remembered being a boy and playing in the street with his two sisters. He remembered his mother, her kindly and smiling face. And the village *imam,* who had been like a father to him since his own father was dead. He had had a pleasant enough boyhood and young adulthood. He regretted nothing from that period of his life.

Things had gotten more serious as he had become older. By then, he was done playing with his sisters and was spending time among friends like himself – boys who were growing like weeds and beginning to resemble, in posture and attitude, grown men. Time spent socializing as a group was fleeting, rare. Before too long, one or the other's fathers had come to collect him for work. They were the sons of herders, of coppersmiths, of traders and subsistence farmers, passing into the ranks and traditions of the family business. But for a boy like Ibrahim, there was no such rite-of-passage.

The cement path curved around the brow of a hill. The sight of the fence and the dead policeman were lost now. It was just him, these rolling green hills and this path.

The White Wolf's men had come to the village when he was 13. On that day, Ibrahim had met Mustafa, the second in command to the White Wolf. He had been cowed by the haughty gaze and commanding mannerisms of the Nigerian enforcer. Ibrahim had been brought into the man's presence along with a group of thirty other boys. Mustafa had studied them all in silence for a considerable period before speaking briefly in a language Ibrahim did not recognize. Neither, apparently, did most of the other boys, for they became distracted, shifting as he spoke. Ibrahim alone had remained in rapt attention. When Mustafa finished speaking, the boys filed out. But a man's hand had dropped to his shoulder, stopping him…

It had been a test, he later learned. Mustafa observed the effect his speech had on prospective recruits to the cause. Boys who paid attention despite not understanding his words were marked as having unusual levels of curiosity and self-control. That day, Ibrahim had distinguished himself.

As he wound around the far edge of the hill and saw the reservoir below, he recalled how it had felt to leave the house of his mother, his friends and the village. He remembered the terrible pain of the goodbye. It was, he realized now, just another of life's many partings.

He pulled the Styrofoam cube from his pocket, opened it and carefully studied the tape securing the stopper to the top of the test tube.

Why don't I just smash the whole thing right away and toss it in? he wondered. To his way of thinking, that made the most sense.

But he had not come this far, survived this long as one of the White Wolf's men by disregarding instructions. Ibrahim Fata prided himself on being a jihadi who followed orders, no matter how difficult. He saw no reason to change that now.

If anything, today it was more important than ever.

And so, there was the past – the village, his family, his boyhood, his recruitment to the cause. And there was today, this time and place. This mission. It was a preliminary blow to what would become Crimson Jihad's final battle with the west. And he, Ibrahim Fata, would be among the jihadis responsible for delivering that blow.

He was close to his goal now. He set his eyes resolutely on the reservoir, the one that supplied drinking water to a third of Athens and bent his steps in that direction. It was now just a matter of time.

He heard police sirens nearby. Snatches of voices could be heard in the distance, perhaps a quarter mile back the way he had come. The policeman's body had been discovered. All well and good. It was too late now.

He did not run. That would be undignified. He merely continued walking, but with a firm stride and much purpose. The first responders would be checking over the prone policeman, assessing his condition, trying to revive him. *That* would take time. As mustering together of the personnel needed for a search party would take time...

He smiled at a memory. Behind their home had been a walled garden where his mother would sometimes send him to pray when he had been disobedient. There had been tile in the walls – ancient and blue. That tile had become the emblem of his impatience. How he despised seeing it, wishing away the moments until he could turn and rejoin the play of his friends, banishing the memory of that tile until next time.

He reached the edge of the reservoir.

In the name of Allah, the compassionate and the merciful...

He knelt and produced his weapons: the Styrofoam cube and the knife. He paused to allow himself a moment of reflection, watching the wavelets scud across the surface of the water, blue like the tile in the garden wall. That sight would be among his final memories.

He opened the cube and lifted out the vial. Then he picked up the knife. He was about to touch the blade to the tape when a bullet vaporized the back of his skull.

———

"DIRECT HIT," said the spotter.

The Greek police sniper cleared the bolt, slotted another round in place and dropped his crosshairs back on the prone figure lying motionless by the reservoir.

"I don't think he's going to move again," confirmed the spotter. "It was a good shot, Aristotle."

The sniper spat. "It was a *perfect* shot," he retorted.

CHAPTER FORTY-NINE

AISHA EMPTIED the clip of the PP-2000 and ceased firing. The Sargo had steamed in circles of ever-decreasing width until she was merely spinning around and around, the momentum from her revolutions drawing her ever closer to the dock. As she figured out how to re-load, the prow of the boat smacked the end of the pier, scraped along its edge and then free again. Upon its next circle, the aft section did the same. Unchecked, the boat would eventually batter itself to pieces on the pier.

She was a bit surprised the gunfire had raised no alarm. But then she reflected on how remote this section of the complex was and that Thelma's Furies were occupied in the firefight against Cody. *If there is an alarm,* she thought, *nobody's monitoring it.*

She replaced the clip and the Sargo's prow smack-dragged the pier again, setting the stern up for another collision. A moment later, she nearly caught a bullet.

BLAM! The dry, flat crack of a pistol sounded from somewhere in the wheelhouse, and the glass window of the bridge cracked. Someone inside was up and firing on her. A second shot came uncomfortably close, causing her to turn and sprint up the pier, chased by bullets. She took refuge behind a waist-high retaining wall and scanned the pier.

Bump…drag…*SMACK*…bump…drag…*SMACK!*

The Sargo's aft hit the pier and a figure jumped off dressed in dark robes and holding a large revolver in his hand. *The White Wolf.* She recognized him instantly.

A fire kindled in her heart, two parts pain to one part pride. This man had caused her family untold suffering, had harassed and targeted their efforts to bring peace to the Middle and Near East and killed Fahd, her favorite uncle. Such a one should inspire fear and dread, and he did. But in Aisha's case, he inspired a cold, cruel sort of rage. The White Wolf was a nobody – a rural Islamic scholar with a power fetish. Her family, meanwhile, came from a royal line. Trained in duty and service, her ancestors had been nobly and conscientiously caring for their people for two centuries. The White Wolf was nothing compared to the power of her royal house. He was less than a servant – less than a *dog*, really. He was a pile of refuse drawing flies outside the backdoor by the servants' entrance. His only claim to authority derived from his willingness to inflict pain and suffering on others.

It was time for that to end.

Now.

Aisha spun into a kneeling position, braced the machine-pistol on the edge of the retaining wall and fired a burst at the exposed figure on the pier. Bullets chopped the water, causing little geysers to rise, and smacked against the stone of the dock, ricocheting off wildly into the high-ceilinged cave. Her first burst sent the White Wolf sprawling to the stone. He returned fire from a prone position, causing her to crouch back behind the wall. Rounds smacked off the brick. Then silence fell.

"Going to try to kill me, hey?" he cried. "You missed! *Sharmuta!*"

She ground her teeth.

He had just called her a whore.

"You and your family! Worse than infidels!" he raged. "You turn on your own! And for what? The almighty American dollar!"

"And, you?" she shot back. "A warrior of Islam? You're an idiot! Dressing up like a 13th century holy man and twisting the Q'uran to whip up hatred! You should be ashamed!"

She heard footsteps. He was coming! She spun back up to her knees, leveled the machine-pistol...and hesitated. He was almost upon her! The two of them fired simultaneously, each succeeding in spooking the other. Aisha ducked back behind her wall. And the White Wolf, gaining the end of the pier, dove and flattened himself behind a stack of crates.

"I look forward to watching you die!" he taunted. "Like your uncle! He was a weakling and a fool, and he deserved a shameful death! And as for your father..."

Wild pain stabbed through her heart. How *dare* he! With the Sheikh's body not yet even cold!

"He will burn in hell fire forever for his betrayal of Islam and his fellow Muslims!"

A madness seized Aisha then – a bloodlust so formidable, it shook her to the core. And suddenly, she was standing outside herself, watching the action unfold...

She stood, leveled the PP-2000 and raked the stack of crates behind which the White Wolf hid. She advanced, screaming, the machine-pistol bucking in her hands, the stench of cordite filling the air as bullets ripped away wood planking and reduced the contents of the crates to dust. Behind this wall of fire she advanced, not caring about her own safety, her will and spirit concentrated into a single imperative: *kill him*.

She stepped around to the side of the crates, ready to claw holes in the White Wolf's body.

But he was *gone*.

A scream from behind her. Then he was smashing her head and shoulders with the heavy revolver. The first blow stunned her, causing her to release her grip on her gun, which clattered to the stones below. She turned, arms raised against the second and caught a glancing blow to the side of her head. Her knees buckled and she wobbled.

The White Wolf chose that moment to grab for her fallen machine-pistol. Aisha steadied herself and kicked out at him as he bent. Her boot connected with the side of his head, causing him to stagger.

Now, she decided, was the moment to run. And she did, taking off back up the hallway to the exit. Behind her came the sound of grunting as the White Wolf pushed himself to his feet and grabbed the gun. Bullets chased her into the shadows.

CHAPTER FIFTY

SARA RUSHED UP to Thelma's desk and scanned the control panel inset into its surface. The red button Thelma had depressed was still winking. Sara hit a switch on the panel and the Mercator projection on the big screen became replaced by a running countdown.

14:59:20... 14:58:57...

"We've got fifteen minutes before this place goes up in smoke." Sara toggled through a series of CCTV images on a small screen beside the desk chair. "Apparently the chateau has charges implanted into the floors, walls, electrical system...even the boiler room is wired to blow."

"Thelma's personal helicopter is parked on the rear balcony. My guess is she'll be headed that way once she rounds up a pilot."

Sara's answering smile was cruel. "Well then we should arrange a reception committee."

"Agreed. Let's find Aisha."

They left through the control room door. Outside, the bodies of dead Furies lay scattered across the marbled concourse. Charred furniture smoked and large chunks were missing from the walls and steps.

"How many more Furies do you think she's got hanging around?"

"Hard to say. She may have brought in reinforcements. And perhaps some of the White Wolf's operatives, as well." He pointed to the steps. "Let's head up."

"Right behind you."

Cody took the shattered steps two at a time, pausing halfway up to avoid a fracture and adjust course. Sara followed suit. They emerged on the landing above and went back-to-back, guns up, scanning the perimeter.

"Clear," said Sara.

"Clear," replied Cody. An otherworldly silence prevailed as wisps of smoke found their way upstairs from below. No Furies. No sign of any staff or Thelma herself. It was as if the two of them were the only souls left alive in the chateau.

"This way," said Cody. And they made it three steps before his cellphone vibrated in his pocket. A text had arrived from an unfamiliar number. He smiled. "It's Aisha. Says she's coming up the main elevator near our rooms."

"Her. Or someone claiming to *be* her," Sara pointed out.

"Let's post up either side of the hallway," he said. "Maximum field of fire on the elevator doors. If it's her, great. If not, we shred them."

"Sounds good."

They hustled through the silent hallways, past the gaudy artwork and plush furniture to the annex where they'd been kept. The elevator doors stood silent, but the

lights on the indicator above showed a car rising: B2…
B1…Ground floor…

Sara sprinted past the doors and sheltered behind a
steel pillar. Cody took up a position on the opposite side,
partially concealed around the edge of the doorway. The
elevator hummed as it slid into place at the floor. The
doors parted and Aisha peeked out.

"Here," Cody said, but kept his gunsights trained on
the doorway in case she wasn't alone.

But she was. And apparently none the worse for
wear. Sara and Cody came forward to greet her.

"Are you okay?" Sara cast a glance over the girl from
head to toe.

"I am, *Allah kareem.*" Aisha hesitated. "He's here. The
White Wolf."

"I'm not surprised," said Cody. "But first things first.
We need to get out of here, and fast. We're heading for
Thelma's chopper. Let's go."

Back through the hallways, back past the gaudy
murals and outlandish décor. Through the atrium with
its glass window giving out onto the Alps Cody could see
columns of smoke from the cooling battle zone rise and
get snatched away by the mountain wind. At Aisha's
urging, they took a hallway that led into an impossibly
large living room. Glass Pella doors looked out onto the
grounds. Cody could see no sign of Thelma or Furies
anywhere.

"Looks like they made themselves scarce," he said.
"How are we on time?"

Sara checked her watch. "Eleven minutes."

The living room led directly into a kitchen. Aisha
pointed to the back door. "That leads out onto the large
patio that surrounds the back end of the house. We can
follow it to the helicopter."

Cody stepped forward, pulled open the door and held it, covering Sara and Aisha as they moved out onto the patio. As Cody moved to follow them, he paused. Sara, attuned to his movements, stopped and turned.

Before she could speak, he held up a hand. Moving his lips to exaggerate his syllables, he mouthed the word: *voices.*

Sara cocked her head. And nodded. Just the faintest trace of voices drifted on the wind. Likely Thelma's staff preparing to bug out by chopper.

Cody held up his gun and raised his eyebrows. Sara, taking his meaning, double-checked her weapon in preparation for what was coming. Aisha, having lost her weapon, stood watching until Sara turned and handed her a pistol. She accepted it gratefully, checked it over and nodded.

It was game time.

Cody led them onto the patio, hugging the walls. This section of the chateau was a windowless wall of piled stone. It curved outward, similar in construction to a turret tower. The voices grew louder as they approached the outer edge of its circumference. And then suddenly all was chaos.

A Fury standing in profile caught sight of Cody and screamed. An instant later, he put her down with a bullet from his Beretta. A hue and cry erupted from somewhere just beyond their field of vision. But then they were around the edge of the tower and staring at their adversaries face-to-face. Thelma Justice and the White Wolf, being escorted amidst a bubble of Furies to the chopper, were among them. All turned toward Cody, Sara and Aisha, the nearest Furies dropping to a knee and raising their weapons.

A fusillade of fire erupted. Sara dove to the ground

and rolled, snapping off shots as she did. Aisha dodged to the right, putting her in the White Wolf's line of sight. He drew his revolver and started toward her as Thelma hit the deck. Then Aisha turned and fled back into the chateau, the White Wolf following. Cody went after them.

They had less than ten minutes remaining.

CHAPTER FIFTY-ONE

CODY RUSHED in through a rear door, what they once would have called a 'service entrance', and emerged into a long, low-ceilinged hallway. The dim shadows ahead – trembling against distant light – were doubtless Aisha and the White Wolf. Cody charged after them, trying to sufficiently narrow the distance between himself and the terrorist to get a clear shot. But this part of the chateau was unfamiliar to him. And the tunnel seemed to grow darker as the distance between overhead bulbs widened.

A shot! Cody considered firing blind but couldn't risk hitting Aisha. They were somewhere up ahead, moving fast into a building that was soon to detonate.

Turning back wasn't an option.

He was going all in.

———

AISHA RAN FASTER than she ever had in her entire life. The slapping sandals and yelled curses of the White Wolf chased her. The mad old man was determined to finish her, as his men had finished her uncle, and she would be damned if she let him get away with it without forcing him to sacrifice his life, too.

If I can lead him deep enough into the chateau, he won't have time to get out and we'll go together, she thought.

It was a decision she reached calmly, rationally. The prospect of her own death did not trouble her. She had spent her life as an observant Muslim. She believed sincerely in her religion, especially its words of compassion. If she succeeded in killing the White Wolf, it would be an act of compassion for the world.

Her life didn't matter. Except for the next few minutes.

A series of narrow doors ran down either side of the corridor. As she reached for one, a shot rang out and splashed into the wall behind her. She yelped, ran and grabbed the next door's handle, yanking it wide and peering in.

A long room, with a doorway at the far end. The vast shadow in the middle?

A dining room table, she thought as she stepped in, yanked the door shut and was delighted to find that *it locked from the inside!* She pressed in and turned the handle, activating the tongue lock before dashing down to the far door, opening it wide and then diving to hide below the table.

———

THE WHITE WOLF skidded to a stop outside the door, yanked at the handle and bellowed in rage. Locked? He pointed the revolver, squeezed the trigger and blasted a hole the size of a soccer ball in the door where the knob had been.

He kicked it wide. The room beyond was dark. But even in the shadows, he could gauge its length and see the open door at the far end. He started toward it …

Then he stopped.

Something in the room was wrong. He couldn't see it. Or even hear it. But he could …

Smell it.

She was here!

He immediately began kicking chairs aside, ripping them from their places at the long dining table and hurling them away. She was here, she was here! He *knew* the smell! Some sort of perfume, some infernal witchery of jasmine donned by *sharmutas* like the little princess to enflame men's passions! He heard her scuttling away from his onslaught. Reaching blindly, grasping under the table he felt her face, then grabbed hold of her hair.

"Come *out!*" he shrieked, yanking. Aisha was hauled out by the bloody roots of her hair, jerked upright and pistol-whipped across the face, hard, with the revolver. She flew partway across the table.

A madness had gripped the White Wolf. He disdained the weapon, dropping it to the floor. He would rip the whore apart with his bare *hands!*

He reached. She intercepted his right forefinger in both hands, jerked forward and then back. It broke. He howled.

And Cody burst through the door.

――――――

CODY HEARD the gunshot blast the knob to smithereens like a thunderclap in the corridor ahead. He heard shouting and the sound of furniture flying. Then Aisha's screams.

The White Wolf had her by the hair and was holding her pinned to the long dining room table. His hand reached for her throat. The look in his eyes made his intentions as plain as a fifty-foot-tall neon sign.

Cody unholstered the Beretta, marched up and placed the muzzle against the White Wolf's left ear.

"Let her go."

The terrorist immediately froze, hand clawed hand inches from Aisha's eyes. The girl, wide-eyed and bursting with adrenalin, did not wait to be told. She slipped free of his grip, slithered down the dining room table to its edge and then down to the floor. And then she was running, as hard and as fast as she could for the chopper.

Cody and the White Wolf stood perfectly still at the center of the room. The terrorist licked his lips and flicked a glance to where Cody still held him at point blank range.

"This place will explode soon," he said. "If we leave now, we can both survive."

"Oh, no. You're not going anywhere." Cody flicked the safety catch of the Beretta to hot. "This is your final resting place."

"Infidel! Murderer!"

"No. *Executioner.* There's a difference. A murderer kills the innocent. An executioner only kills the guilty. And I pronounce you guilty. In the name of the civilized world and all the good people of all faiths who inhabit it. You'll never live to poison another life, another nation, another mind and heart ever again. I pronounce sentence on you in the name of the president and Congress as a war criminal and enemy of the United States of America. Judgment: guilty. The sentence will be carried out immediately."

He fired. The Beretta roared. The White Wolf's skull cratered, and the terrorist collapsed in a heap of blood-spattered robes. And then Cody was off and running as fast as he could.

Less than six minutes remained.

CHAPTER FIFTY-TWO

THIS IS IT, Sara thought. *This is where I die.*

These thoughts came to her calmly, without alarm. Not born of fear, they were rather the product of a careful analysis of her situation. The analysis happened instantaneously – she had, after all, been CIA for a long time. But it was no less thorough for its speed, nor less conclusive in its findings.

Fact: she was alone in an open space without cover facing a small force of trained paramilitary armed with semi-automatic weapons.

There was nothing she could do to avoid their fire save jump off the balcony. And it was a thousand-foot drop to the bottom.

And so she thought through what she had to do now. Maximize her chances for survival for as long as possible. Draw out the engagement and pin down as many of the enemy's resources as she could. Kill as many of them as she can in the time left to her.

Cody will have that many less to face when he emerges, she thought.

She thought all these things in a split-second. Of all these things and of the face of the man she loved, who was nearby.

Goodbye, Jack, she thought.

In a single fluid motion, she drew her sidearm, fell forward into a prone firing position, absorbing the shock of her fall with her biceps and chest as she had been trained to do. The stone floor stung on impact, but it focused her. Her first three shots were direct hits. The small party guarding Thelma and the chopper began to break ranks. One or two of them maintained their posts, adjusting their fire. Sara shot them next.

Thelma. More than anything, she wanted to get to Thelma.

But the momma bear of the operation was out of sight. Now the bodies of dead Furies obscured the view even further. And the gunfire was creeping close to where she lay. So she rolled, adjusted her angle and kept firing.

A deep thrumming filled the air.

At first, she didn't register the sound. But when she saw Thelma Justice rise from where she was crouched behind her chopper, Sara noted the woman looked skyward. The gunfire fell silent as, one by one, the surviving Furies did likewise.

Sara turned, too.

A cloud of dark shapes was blocking the sun. When the thrumming rose in tone and became the whine of rotors, she understood what she was seeing. It was a squadron of choppers. Squinting against the glare, she recognized Italian military insignia.

The aircraft came in low, in staggered formation. Some of the Furies began firing on the choppers but ducked for cover when the pilots returned fire with sixty-millimetre chain guns. Force of impact crushed brick, pierced metal and blew out the nearest windows of the chateau. The Furies scattered, taking cover beneath Thelma's helicopter or behind the low wall surrounding the rear doors. The Italian military birds swooped low, their skids barely two meters from the deck when the side doors rolled open.

Troops disembarked and immediately engaged the Furies. Sara's trained eye immediately recognized special operations forces. These guys were good, no-nonsense operators. They swiftly cut a beachhead into the resisting shooters. That's when Sara recognized that the soldiers were dark-skinned and sporting Emirati patches. Now it was a pitched battle on the stone landing zone, Emirati special forces against Thelma's private army.

Suddenly, Thelma herself broke from the chopper and made for the doorway.

Sara raised her pistol, squeezed the trigger and heard the pin click into an empty chamber. She tossed the gun aside and went after Thelma barehanded.

Sara crashed into her mid-section, blindsiding her. Thelma's legs went out from under her, and they crashed together onto hard stone. Sara kept a grip on Thelma's coat, climbing up the struggling body until she straddled her and sending a few well-aimed punches to the chin.

"It's over!" Sara screamed. "Vetrov's dead! Your control room is destroyed! Your army is defeated!"

"Go to hell," Thelma snarled through bloodied lips. And arched suddenly, knocking Sara sideways and doing a credible sweep. She came out on top, a knife in her right fist. Sara's right wrist was pinned to the deck by Thelma's left. Her drop-sheath with its razor-honed throwing knife was at her right wrist. Inaccessible.

Thelma's knife swept downward. There came a sudden blur of movement and blast of impact. Aisha hurtled forward, threw a running leg kick and knocked Thelma sideways. Her knife went clattering across stone.

"Aisha!"

There, across the patio, stood her brother, His Excellency, Sheikh Achmed attired in an Emirati special operations uniform and holding an SMG. He strode toward them through the now becalmed battle-zone. Thelma's helicopter was a shredded wreck. Her security force had been annihilated. Only the woman herself remained, bloodied, soot-streaked and wild-eyed with rage.

"We have to get clear, Your Majesty!" cried Sara. "This place is about to blow!"

Achmed nodded, produced a whistle and gave three sharp shrieks. At once, the choppers lowered themselves close enough without touching down to allow troops to begin boarding.

"What about her?" Aisha pointed.

Thelma Justice had clambered to her knees. She remained there, under the guns of two of Achmed's men.

Cody burst through the doorway and onto the patio. Sara's face exploded into a wide grin.

"We're about to blow!" he cried.

"Into the choppers!" Achmed waved his gun and began retreating toward his own helicopter.

"C'mon." Cody grabbed Aisha's bicep in one hand and Sara's in the other. Across the balcony, Thelma Justice had wobbled to her feet.

They had nearly reached the helicopter when Sara turned back in time to see Thelma stoop and reach for a dead Fury's machine-gun. Before the woman could raise it, Sara snatched the Beretta from Cody's holster, spun and fired.

The round smashed Thelma's right knee to powder, causing the woman to buckle to the stone, screaming.

The gun she had recovered spun from her grasp, landing out of reach.

"How long now?" Sara asked.

Cody checked his watch. "Just over a minute."

Sara nodded, turned and boarded the nearest helicopter. Aisha did likewise and Cody followed. A moment later, they were rising away from the balcony patio toward the peaks above.

Thelma Justice pulled herself into position to watch them go. The hate that rose within her was volcanic – almost painful in its passion. But she did not have to endure it for long. Within moments, the first of the shaped charges detonated. The front windows of the chateau blew out in a gust of fire and light. With a crack, the supporting beams of the second floor gave way and the stone collapsed. All around her, everything began to burn as her Alpine chateau began its descent into chaos.

CHAPTER FIFTY-THREE

THE CHOPPERS MADE their way across the Alps to a small airbase a dozen or so miles from the chateau. There they were met by an Italian air force general and a representative of the defense ministry, who greeted Sheikh Achmed with extravagant courtesy. Cody noted enormous changes in Aisha's brother as he accepted their greetings and gave a brief summary of events at the chateau. Gone was the ruthless and impatient man that had moved hell and Earth in pursuit of his sister. Now that he enjoyed singular authority over his nation and subjects, Achmed seemed relaxed. Generous, even.

He's become magnanimous, Cody realized. It was a good look for royalty, and Achmed wore it well.

The general conducted them to a conference room in one of the airbase's administration buildings. There, Sheikh Achmed took a seat at the head of the table and invited Aisha, Cody and Sara to do likewise with a sweep of his hand. An Emirati officer attended Achmed, who turned and ordered refreshments brought in. The officer saluted and departed to fetch them.

"Jack Cody and Sara Durell," said Sheikh Achmed, as he stretched and relaxed back into his chair. "I owe the two of you my apologies. For the longest time, it was my belief that you had kidnapped my dear sister, the princess. I have since learned better. Forgive me."

He turned to his sister.

"And you, dear sister. Please forgive your brother and king. I sought only to follow the instructions of our late father."

"Peace be upon him," she whispered, tears clouding her eyes.

"Peace be upon him," agreed Achmed. "He rests now in Paradise. And it remains for us to build on his legacy." He turned to Cody and Sara. "We intend to continue and strengthen our alliance with our friends in the United States. I have a call with President Harwood scheduled for later this week. We will continue to lay the groundwork for the summit meeting the late sheikh and he were working on. And, unofficially, we will work behind the scenes for greater cooperation between our military and intelligence services and your CIA."

Cody smiled. "I'm sure the director will be pleased to hear that."

"We'll do everything we can to help, Your Majesty," promised Sara.

"Will you?" Sheikh Achmed cracked a smile. "I was hoping you would say that."

At this, Aisha laughed. "I know the look on His Majesty's face," she chuckled. "My friends, you have walked into a trap."

Sheikh Achmed exploded in laughter. "If it is a trap, then it is a very luxurious one," he hastened to add.

"What's the angle here?" Cody cocked an eyebrow.

"Surely, we haven't caused some sort of diplomatic incident...?"

"Far from it." Sheikh Achmed cleared his throat. "Jack Cody and Sara Durell. Because of your position as secret agents, you are unable to receive official American government recognition for your efforts. But that does not forbid you from receiving the thanks of foreign governments.

"As Sheikh, I am honored to invite you to the Emirates. You will stay at the palace as my honored guests. We will have a banquet in your honor, and you will be recognized as heroes of our nation and personal friends of its royal family." He tipped a nod to Aisha. "All of this will be conducted in secret or under proper pretexts to maintain your anonymity. To outsiders, you will appear as innocent representatives of an NGO receiving the sheikh's favor. But the truth will be known to us. And to your president."

Cody considered this all carefully. Sheikh Achmed was right – he and Sara were not allowed to receive any sort of official recognition for their work. But the circumstances here – the gravity of the mission they had just completed, the advent of Achmed's reign as sheikh and their rescue of Aisha conspired to make this invitation unusual in the extreme.

"Your Majesty, we accept." Cody smiled. "So long as it's kept under the rug, we'd be honored to receive Emirati recognition."

"Excellent!" Achmed clapped his hands. "All will held in greatest secrecy, I assure you. I took the liberty of clearing it with the president personally. You have his full support."

"Thank you," said Sara.

"And you will be there to witness another recognition." Achmed turned to Aisha. "It is long past time for our kingdom to recognize another of its great treasures."

"The Marian Fragment," said Aisha. "You received it?"

Sheikh Achmed nodded. "Safely transferred to our ambassador in Zurich. He saw it sent home. But that is not the treasure of which I speak."

Aisha looked startled.

"To be sure, it will receive pride of place in our historical displays, but..." He raised his hands. "We have no national museum. This is an oversight that must be corrected. Especially for so great a treasure. The time has come to establish a foundation dedicated to historical scholarship. The Fragment must be available to scholars from all nations and faiths. Such an undertaking will require courage. Leadership. And a unique talent for courting the academic world."

Slow understanding began to dawn on Aisha's face.

"A project of such national importance cannot be left to commoners." Achmed shrugged. "It is my intention to see to it that the museum is firmly established with royal blessings as the custodian of our national story. It must, and shall, be overseen by a member of the royal family.

"And so, dear sister, it is my honor to install you as the Chief Executive Officer and head of the Board of Directors of the National Museum of the Emirates. Your task shall be to design and build a museum fitting for such a great historical legacy. You have proven your courage and dedication to both our nation and religion by your efforts these past weeks. Will you take on this task for your brother and king?"

Aisha looked to Cody and Sara, then back to her brother again.

"It would be my great honor, Your Majesty," she whispered. There were tears in her eyes.

CHAPTER FIFTY-FOUR

MEANWHILE, an identical story was unfolding in cities across the world...

In Berlin, a maid knocked on a hotel room door. Except that she was not a maid but a special officer of GSG 9, the counterterrorism response unit of the German Federal Police Force. The door opened just the tiniest fraction and she began speaking with the guest inside. By his facial expression, it was obvious he understood none of what she said, but that didn't matter. She managed to distract him long enough for the SWAT team to rappel down the outside of the building and smash through the hotel room windows while his back was turned. As he spun, she and three other officers smashed through the door and pinned him face-first to the rug, the muzzle of a machine-gun at his ear as his hands were cuffed and a canvas hood pulled over his head. A hazmat team entered and began tossing the room as he was dragged out to a waiting service elevator.

In Ottawa, two Canadian Security and Intelligence agents watched as a room service meal was delivered to the door of a man who had been staying at the hotel for two weeks, never venturing from his room. The meal tray was left outside the door. After a time, the door opened and the man dragged the tray inside, locking the door behind him. The CSIS agents checked the time. Five minutes later, they entered the room to find the man passed out at the writing desk, face down in the plate of drugged pasta specially prepared for him by a lab in the Defence Ministry. After checking his vital signs to ensure he had not succumbed to an overdose, they called the paramedics and had the unconscious man restrained to a stretcher. Within minutes, he was bundled onboard a van for a private appointment with an interrogator in the basement of the CSIS building, where the accommodations were significantly less hospitable.

In Paris, the man who had been residing quietly at the Hilton for the past two weeks went against instructions and left his room, taking the elevator down to the lobby to purchase some candy bars at the gift shop. His journey was unremarked by any save a handful of undercover agents from the GIGN, France's elite police counterterrorism unit. One was onboard the elevator car when he returned and pushed the button for his destination on the sixth floor. At the second, the car stopped and a second GIGN agent entered, pretending to be engrossed in a newspaper. Two more, disguised as a married couple, entered on four. When the doors parted on the sixth floor, a group of uniformed policemen waited, led by a smiling man who spoke fluent Arabic. He suggested that, because it was a long drop to the sidewalk outside, the man come quietly with them. Fortunately, he did.

In a New York hotel room, the man dispatched by the White Wolf sighed, stretched and shuffled to the washroom, a towel over his arm. Accustomed to roughing it in the Syrian desert, he derived almost sensual pleasure from the presence of a working bathtub and an unlimited supply of hot water. Knowing he would die soon, he indulged himself in two baths per day, a fact not lost on the operatives of the U.S. Army's Delta Force. The man had just adjusted the temperature of the bathwater to his liking and was relaxing back in the tub when they cut the power to his room. He was still wondering why the lights had gone out when the bathroom door was kicked open and he became enmeshed in a web of red laser dots and the spectral green glow of night vision gear. Naked, he was hauled from the tub, handcuffed and blindfolded before being hustled from the room for an appointment with an FBI interrogator.

In Moscow, a group of FSB agents huddled around a video monitor in the basement of the Holiday Inn. Over the course of the past 12 hours, a series of tiny digital surveillance cameras had been installed in the room via careful insertion from neighboring rooms or by agents posing as hotel staff. As they watched, their target put out the lights and crawled into bed. The Russian agents sat motionless as the minutes ticked by. When audio surveillance picked up the soft sound of his snoring, they moved, taking the elevator up to his floor and entering the room with a skeleton key. When they shook him awake, he opened his eyes to the muzzles of six submachineguns trained on him at point-blank range.

A man in a dark trench coat, an FSB colonel, entered the room and pushed his way through the assembled agents to study the man at close range. The colonel sneered. Taking the measure of the terrorist, he doubted the man would last an hour under close interrogation.

He barked an order, and the crew handcuffed the man, swaddled him in his own bedclothes and dumped him into a wheeled hamper, that they brought by elevator to the basement parking garage. The colonel watched as the hamper was wheeled into a police van and driven away. Once the van was gone, the colonel returned to his Zil limousine, which was parked near the entrance to the parking garage. Getting in, he spoke in English to the man sharing the backseat with him.

"He is in our hands, thanks to you." The colonel smiled. "The Russian Federation is indebted to you."

"Oh, not at all," said Horace Parsons with a chuckle. "Least I could do, old chap."

CHAPTER FIFTY-FIVE

THE RETURN of Sheikh Achmed and the Princess Aisha to the Emirates was a celebrated public affair. News correspondents from a dozen nations waited on the tarmac as the royal jet landed. They jostled for position as the pair appeared at the top of the stairway and descended to the long red carpet where an honor guard waited. The soldiers snapped to attention, arms presented as the sheikh moved to the podium to address the press.

"My friends, it is with great joy that we observe the return of our dear sister, the Princess Aisha to our kingdom. Over the next few days, the story of her journey will be told." He paused and smiled. "They say Sinbad had many dangerous voyages in his time. I daresay the name of Princess Aisha will one day join his as a great hero of the Middle East. She has done our royal house and our kingdom heroic service that is recognized not only by ourselves but also by the President of the United States. In the coming days, we will also announce new initiatives and projects between ourselves and America, cementing a new era of friendship and cooperation between our two countries. We have our sister to thank for this development. Our entire kingdom owes her a debt of gratitude."

Achmed finished, observed by Cody and Sara, who remained onboard the royal jet until the press departed. Then, with great courtesy, they were conducted down to a waiting limousine. Under military escort, they were driven to the palace where a suite of apartments had been set aside for them.

"Look at this!" Sara enthused, dropping her backpack on the couch and looking around. "This place has more square footage than my condo in Aspen."

"It's gorgeous," agreed Cody. He went to the window and pushed aside the curtains. Outside, a swimming pool glimmered on the wide balcony. He went to Sara and took her into his arms. "This is sort of like the end of one of those ridiculous spy movies."

"Isn't this where we're supposed to make mad love while our bosses try fruitlessly to contact us?" Sara laughed and kissed his cheek. She led him through the doorway to the bedroom with its massive, canopied bed.

"My God, this is luxurious," said Cody, kicking off his shoes and climbing onto the duvet. "This thing feels like a cloud."

Sara followed suit, doffing her sneakers and climbing in to snuggle up beside him. Cody was about to reply to her quip about making love while the phone rings off the hook until he noticed that she was snoring softly.

They had been through a lot.

It was time to rest.

A PRIVATE BANQUET, attended only by members of the royal family, was held in their honor. Cody and Sara were introduced to the top civil servants in the country, most of whom were relatives of Achmed and Aisha. Before the banquet began, they were called to rise and present themselves before Sheikh Achmed.

"It is a rare honor to bestow this award," he said solemnly. "It is normally reserved for visiting heads of state. Because of your status of operatives of US intelligence, we give this award in the deepest secrecy. But it is no less heartfelt for that."

He turned to a waiting attendant. From the pillow in the attendant's hands, the sheikh lifted a heavily ornamented chain from which hung an ornate, seven-pointed star. He stepped toward Cody.

"I invest you with the Emirates' highest civilian honor – the Order of Zayed. I do this in the name of the Emirati people, and on behalf of a grateful nation."

Cody bowed his head ,and the sheikh slipped the medal around his neck. Sara was next. Cody was surprised to see a glimmer of tears rimming her eyes as she stepped back.

"It's amazing to serve your own country," she whispered, "but when you can do that and serve the world? It's…"

Cody nodded and smiled. He understood.

Over the course of the next hour and a half, Cody consumed more good food than he thought humanly possible. The delicacies were endless, and not only Middle Eastern in origin. Sara went crazy on the dolmathes. Cody was surprised to discover how much he liked goat.

Later, the banquet done and its guests departed, Sheikh Achmed and Aisha brought them to a secluded room of the palace guarded by an armed soldier. He snapped to attention as the sheikh arrived and tapped a code into an electronic lock. A door slid aside to reveal a darkened chamber. The sole object within was illuminated in a bright shaft of silver light.

"The Marian Fragment," said Sheikh Achmed. "Recovered at last."

Aisha gave a heavy sigh of relief.

Sara stepped forward to examine the small object that had been the cause of so much trouble. It was a simple clay rectangle, about the size of a pocket calculator. Bending forward, she squinted at the tiny characters impressed into its surface.

"That whole story about Jesus is here?" she asked. "On this tiny thing?"

Aisha laughed. "In the ancient world, good quality papyrus and clay were difficult to find. Our forebears knew how to write in small, neat lettering. Especially the Jews! Why, there is a famous case of an early version of the Torah that…"

"My sister the expert." Achmed laid a hand on her shoulder. "You must tell us all about it over coffee and dessert."

"As the head of our new national museum, it would be my honor," replied Aisha with a chuckle.

Cody studied the tablet for a long moment. It was a version of the Jesus story that would rock the world. He was glad it was safe in the hands of a progressive, educated ruler like Achmed.

"It's strange to think Jesus might have had a sister," he said. "That's a very different story from the one I was raised on."

"But it's not all that weird," said Sara, coming forward and taking his hand. "Men and women were meant to work together. No one sex should dominate. We're at our best when we cooperate."

"Agreed." He smiled.

"We agree as well," affirmed Achmed. "When the two halves of humanity labor together in harmony, all is well. How can the future they create together be anything but bright?"

Cody nodded. He couldn't help but agree.

CHAPTER FIFTY-SIX

"ONCE YOU GIVE THE WORD, Mr. President," said the chairman of the joint chiefs, "we can start the clock on Operation WHIRLWIND. All the final preparations have been completed. Withdrawal from Afghanistan will be accomplished with lightning speed, sir."

"And the risk to our people is minimal?" President Martin Harwood, in shirtsleeves with tie loosened, stared morosely out the darkened windows of the Oval Office toward the Rose Garden.

"Yes, sir," said the chairman. "Surprise. Speed. Operational security. Our people will be gone before the Taliban even knows what happened."

The president nodded. "I appreciate everything you and the general staff have done on this, Mr. Chairman. Believe me…withdrawing our troop presence from that country after twenty years is necessary, but…I can't help feeling for those we'll be leaving behind."

"Yes, sir," the chairman spoke softly. "A great many Afghans rallied to our cause, aided our troops, worked on our bases and in our embassies. Any left behind when we pull out will be in grave danger."

"And yet…" Harwood turned and took a seat behind the Resolute desk. "Our troops have reached the breaking point. Years of operational stagnation, plummeting morale, interference from NGOs…a few questionable commanders… We have to think of them, of our own people, first. Alright, Mr. Chairman. Pass along instructions to our commanders to prep for WHIRLWIND and immediate egress from the country on my order. I'll be down in the Situation Room to give that order shortly. But there's something I need to deal with here, first."

"Yes, sir. We'll be ready."

The president waited until the chairman had gone before hitting the intercom switch to the chief of staff's office. "You have them assembled?" he asked.

"Yes, Mr. President," answered the chief of staff. "I've got them here."

"Okay. Stand by." The president hit the switch to contact his secretary. "Okay. Send him in."

Harwood stood and shrugged into his jacket, pausing to straighten his tie in the reflection from a darkened windowpane before turning. The door opened and Jared Parnell entered. Parnell had visited the Oval several times in the past. The president could tell that he viewed himself as someone indispensable, someone with the coveted "access" that so many craved. Inexplicably sidelined in recent days, he was now returning to the center of the action – his preferred locale, believing (no doubt) that his exile was over. From his breezy smile and crisp step, one might imagine he was preparing to receive the Congressional Medal of Honor.

"You wanted to see me, Mr. President?"

Harwood turned, hands behind his back, and measured Parnell with a long and penetrating glare before speaking.

"You will be pleased to learn that General Vetrov is dead," he said. "So is Thelma Justice. As part of the same operation, we have captured or killed all surviving members of Crimson Jihad, including the White Wolf himself. A major global biowarfare attack has been prevented and the nuclear terror threat has been eliminated. We won. But it was a close-run thing."

"Yes, sir." Parnell smiled. "CIA was only too glad to be of service."

Harwood paused, his jaw firming.

"Langley's role in this has been limited," the president replied. "Much of it has been coordinated through this office. Personally. By me. Final success, however, was achieved in the field. Thanks to Jack Cody and Sara Durell."

"Sir, Cody has been a loose cannon now for years. And Sara Durell is—"

"One of the finest agents CIA has ever produced! A national resource of incalculable strategic value. As is Cody." Harwood crossed his arms. "Jared, I know you're ambitious. Being competitive is an asset in your line of work. But that shouldn't extend to undermining your fellow agents. You've been placing roadblocks in Cody's way from the beginning. And your attempt to sideline Sara Durell was—"

"Absolutely necessary, sir, in the name of secur—"

"Brutally careerist and self-interested. You derailed important agency work, undermined our campaign against a global terror threat and worked to sideline two of our top people continuously throughout so…what? So you could reap the rewards and step into first place on the medal rostrum?" Harwood shook his head angrily. "This isn't a goddam swim meet! We're protecting a nation – and, increasingly, a united world. There's no place for the kind of *bullshit* you've been bringing to the table! You're a snake, Parnell. A self-interested, ruthless asshole who undermines his betters and steals other men's work to present as his own. And what I cannot – *will* not – forgive is that your efforts put our country in danger."

He marched to the desk and hit the intercom switch to the chief of staff's office.

"Send them in, please."

A side door in the office wall opened and three men entered. Soberly dressed and carrying themselves with the diffidence demanded by their surroundings, they were as different from one another as it was possible for three men to be. But their unity of purpose and confidence showed through. The man who led them, a diminutive Brit in round glasses, nodded to the president.

"I'd like you to meet the senior members of the Backchannel network, Jared." President Harwood smiled thinly. "Horace Parsons, Hamid Hassan and Hiroto Ishigawa. All three are retired members of allied intelligence services. And all three have a bone to pick with you."

Parnell's eyes widened and he blanched visibly.

"You're going to go with them," Harwood concluded. "I have authorized these guys to review Agency activity with each of their parent services with a view to identifying any areas you may have compromised through your relentless careerism. They'll be doing this at one of our black sites. And when they're done, you'll be taking an extended leave of absence from CIA." He fixed

Parnell with a stare. "I recommend you start looking for your next job, Jared."

Parnell's composure disintegrated in slow stages. No longer able to maintain the façade of a high-flying government professional, his facial expression slackened. His shoulders drooped. And his hand went reflexively to his pocket and emerged holding his vape pen. He raised it to his lips.

"Ah, Jared?" The president smiled. "This is a US federal workplace. There's no smoking or vaping in the Oval Office."

EPILOGUE

Kandahar Airbase, Afghanistan

"ANY WORD?"

"No, sir."

"Damn!" The captain banged his fist on the desk. Visible through the office window was the last US Air Force C-130 idling on the tarmac containing the last cohort of US military personnel waiting to be evacuated from Afghanistan as part of Operation WHIRLWIND. The captain had served three tours in-country, had learned to love the locals and believe in the mission. He did not want to leave. But orders were orders.

Turning to the enlisted radio operator, he said, "Try them again."

"Sir." The sergeant bent forward and hit the mic switch. "This is Kilo-One to Evac Echo-Six. Come in Echo-Six."

He released the mic switch. A wave of static washed through the radio room speakers.

"Kilo-One to Evac chopper Echo-Six. This is a Priority Delta call. Come in Echo-Six!"

Again, the mic switch release, and more static. But swimming within the dissonance, the captain caught the faint words *echo* and *trouble*. He put a hand on the sergeant's shoulder.

"Switch to alternate frequency and boost the gain. C'mon, son!"

"Sir!" The sergeant's fingers flew over his ops panel. The static warbled, lessened and cleared. The chopper pilot's voice came through faintly but clearly:

"Kilo-One, this is Echo-Six!" The pilot was female. Her voice cut through the remaining static smoothly. "We are forty kilometers out and losing altitude! Fast! I am about to make an emergency landing!"

Jesus! thought the captain. Of all the times for this to happen...

"Get a fix on their location and tell them to stand by," said the captain. Then he turned and sprinted out the door and across the tarmac to the waiting C-130. The sun was hot and the air, still and dry. The drone of the idling C-130 filled his ears as he approached the lone figure in a bulletproof vest and helmet standing by the airplane's open ramp. The captain stopped short of the figure and saluted.

"General!" he shouted through the din. "We have a downed rescue chopper! Forty clicks north of our position! Last evac out of that sector!"

The general tilted his helmeted head to listen through the engine noise. Then, turning, he beckoned for another soldier to take his place guarding the ramp before following the captain back into the radio room.

"Sir, we've got their position." The radio operator tore a top sheet from a notepad and handed it across.

"They're in Indian country, sir. Down and taking fire as we speak."

The captain scanned the coordinates on the page before offering it to the general. Who shook his head.

"I'm sorry, son," he said. "I'd lead the rescue mission personally if we weren't under orders. Commander in chief has been crystal clear on this one."

"But, sir. Surely…"

"No." The general shook his head firmly. "Operational orders are clear. WHIRLWIND is on the clock and is to be run by the numbers. No ifs, ands or buts. Echo-Six is a casualty of war."

The captain and the sergeant looked at each other and then back at the general.

"Yes, sir," said the captain quietly.

The general swallowed. "Both of you. Out to the plane. Now."

The two men gathered up their gear and double-timed it to the C-130. The general watched as they hit the ramp and dashed inside. Apart from the crew of Echo-Six, he was now the last US serviceman in Afghanistan.

He stepped forward and pushed the mic button.

"Echo-Six, this is General Edwin Daniels. We have no choice but to abandon our position here. We cannot – repeat, *cannot* – send help at this time. Your sit-rep is noted and will be relayed up the chain of command. I'm…I'm sorry. God speed."

Every fibre in the general's body rebelled against leaving men behind. More than anything, he wanted to gather a crew, board any one of the dozens of choppers they were planning to abandon on base and go after Echo-Six. But that was out of the question.

Orders were orders.

And goddam if he didn't hate them with a passion just now.

He was almost at the door when the radio crackled again.

"General Daniels…"

The voice was male, and undeniably foreign. He stopped and turned back. Stabbing the mic switch, he snapped: "Who is this?"

After a lengthy stream of static, the voice answered:

"This is the man who has captured your helicopter. And crew. Thank you for reassuring us there will be no rescue. We promise a merciful death for your countrymen."

Daniels fought an uncontrollable shiver of rage that pulsed through his body. Thirty years of service and experience in four different wars had hardened him into a fighting machine of rare capability. But right now, it was all he could do to fight back tears.

Outside, the roar of the C-130's engines rose to a fever pitch. It was time to go.

He stepped forward and stabbed the mic switch.

"As God is my witness, I'll see you strung up, you son-of-a-bitch," Daniels spat.

"Brave words from the American dog who tucks his tail and runs, like so many before him." The voice laughed.

"We may be leaving," Daniels replied. "But so long as you hold American service personnel, this isn't over. Payback is coming. And where I come from, we have a saying."

"And what is that?"

"Payback's a bitch," snarled Daniels. Then he released the mic switch, turned and sprinted through the doorway to the waiting plane.

PAYBACK!

America's disorganized military evacuation from the Hell on Earth called Afghanistan left ace CIA field agent Jack Cody with a bitter, dissatisfied fire in his gut. Maybe it was strategically viable, but too much good was being left undone in a country that had fallen into wholesale slaughter and savagery following America's withdrawal.

Now, the Taliban is in power, and no one is safe.

But when the US government learns that a handful of American military personnel may have been left behind and are being held prisoner by a cruel Taliban warlord somewhere in that godforsaken country, nothing can stop the man they call Suicide Cody from launching a one-man dark-op mission to locate their people and bring them home . . . or die trying!

From Stephen Mertz, the modern master of action-adventure novels, comes this hard-hitting saga of combat and heroism.

"Stephen Mertz is a Grandmaster of action/adventure!"

—MensAdventureMagazine&Books.com

AVAILABLE MAY 2022

ABOUT THE AUTHOR

Stephen Mertz is an American fiction author who is best known for his mainstream thrillers and novels of suspense. His work covers a wide variety of styles from paranormal dark suspense (*Night Wind* and *Devil Creek*) to historical speculative thrillers (*Blood Red Sun*) and hardboiled noir (*Fade to Tomorrow*). Mertz is also a popular lecturer on the craft of writing and has appeared as a guest speaker before writer's groups and at universities.

During high school and college, Steve regularly scandalized his "literary, well-intentioned" creative writing teachers with "thud and blunder melodramas." Throughout military service, travel, and a wide variety of jobs, his goal remained to become a publishing, full-time freelance professional. "It was never a question for me of if, but always when." His first national sale was to a mystery magazine, and his first novel, a detective thriller entitled *Some Die Hard*, was published under the pseudonym of Stephen Brett. Another Brett novel followed, as did a string of mystery and suspense short stories.

Steve's writing output increased dramatically when he emerged as one of the country's most in-demand writers of adventure paperback novels, averaging four books per year for ten years. His work on Don Pendleton's Mack Bolan series is regarded by fans as some of the best in that series. He also created the Mark Stone:

MIA Hunter and Cody's Army series, written under the pseudonyms Jack Buchanan and Jim Case respectively.

Stephen Mertz has traveled widely and is a U.S. Army veteran. He presently lives in the American Southwest, and he is always at work on a new book.